LELAND STEWART

An Irish Love Affair

Pam,
meeting you & Mike was the highlight of
my day! I hope to see you again soon.

Best regards,
— Leland Stewart
"Boyd"

ST. FINIAN'S PRESS
Dallas, Texas

ISBN: 1497402581
ISBN-13: 9781497402584

For information, address:

Leland Stewart
St Finian's Press
11700 Preston Road
Suite 660 - 174
Dallas, TX 75230

Library of Congress Cataloging in Publication Data

An Irish Love Affair: A Second Chance at Love
— a novel / Leland Stewart — 1st edition

1. Stewart, Leland, 2012

2. Divorced people — fiction

3. Romance-mid life — fiction

4. Ireland — fiction

5. Annapolis — fiction

Dedicated to the women and relationships we fortunate men have experienced. Some fail miserably, but each has moments of incredible beauty, softness, nurturing, passion, and growth. Truly Hammerstein was right —

"There's Nothing Like A Dame"

There is nothin' like a dame,
Nothin' in the world,
There is nothin' you can name
That is anythin' like a dame!

— Oscar Hammerstein II
"South Pacific" 1949

And most of all to:

Gracie
The best friend a man could
ever have

December 2, 2013

Driving to Craggy Rock Lodge
Connemara, County Galway Ireland
September 2009

CHAPTER 1
On The Edge

⚬❧

Europe in late September is sublime. The weather usually cooperates with warm days and crisp nights, the tourists are gone, and the cripplingly expensive costs for summer visitors fall back into line. Exhausted by months of unrelieved stress and long hours in my quest for more and more – business, customers, accounts – all the stuff that seemed so important these last four years, I just folded my briefcase that Thursday, threw the office keys to my secretary Charlene, and left.

It had been such a struggle to get the business off the ground, make payroll every week, and stay out of bankruptcy court. Four years with no personal life, scarcely a day off, except for an occasional Sunday, no softness from a special woman, no one to confide in that I trusted (more than I did Charlene)... no break, no respite for four years.

Retired Captain Harold Whitson, M.D., my classmate from college days at Annapolis and currently my physician, had given me an ultimatum – take some time off or he would have me involuntarily committed (with the help of my father) to one of his favorite income streams – a psychiatric hospital. Harold was such an overachiever – Naval Officer, F-18 carrier pilot, medical doctor, husband of the most beautiful woman in the world, and father of two world class children – I loved him, but hated him more. He had everything I had always wanted. Now as my best friend, he seemed serious about his threat to collaborate with my father to put me away for a few weeks.

"Charlene, you're in charge! If Southwest Designs can't be run by you for the next few weeks, then it doesn't deserve to survive. Write the memo, let me sign it, give a copy to Harold and one to Dave (my other Annapolis roommate — a lawyer and a man who makes Bill Clinton look like a celibate priest)." That was it – I walked out and told no one where I was going. I locked my laptop, cellular phone, and pager in the car parked in the garage at home.

Craggy Rock Lodge

How little did I realize what the next 72 hours would bring as I drove down the winding lane toward the converted hunting lodge. Craggy Rock Lodge – in the guidebook, it sounded quaint, restful, out of the way, and with enough masculinity to suit me. It's funny now, how serendipitous was the selection – this week in time, a never-heard-of-before place, 240 miles away from the Dublin airport in the northwest corner of Connemara in Ireland – just sheer, dumb, blind luck that was to change my life forever.

As I came to the end of the lane, there appeared a place of such beauty as to briefly take your breath away. Craggy Rock Lodge, perched on a low bluff and separated from a picture perfect cove by a small meadow filled with wildflowers – it was as if Disney designed it – just too quaint to be real. It had been a long time since the romantic side of me had surfaced, but this evening with the Lodge's lights just starting to come on, the trees, lawn, and plantings bathed in the final rays of late afternoon sun, and a friendly, well-behaved collie waiting by the front door, I felt a lump in my throat – I had been out of touch with beauty for far too long.

"Good evening, Mr. Harte. I am Cathleen O'Doyle. Welcome to the Craggy Rock Lodge." Mrs. O'Doyle, like seemingly everything else connected with the property, was stunning, a woman in maybe her late 40's. According to the guidebook, she and her husband Reginald Exall had spent the last 12 years converting the property from rustic hunting lodge to a simple, but rather elegant country house hotel out in this remote part of the county. She was Irish and had inherited the Lodge from her family, keeping her maiden name as the last of the O'Doyles. "We have you staying with us for five days, is that correct?"

"If the food is good and the library well stocked, I may stay for a second week. What would you say to that? Are you filled?"

"No, sir. We have only a couple celebrating their 50th wedding anniversary, a few tourists from Germany on holiday, and a single lady from Pennsylvania in the United States like yourself. Is Pennsylvania near your home of Dallas?"

After a brief lesson in U.S. geography with Cathleen, I asked for the quietest room she had available and made my way towards it, upstairs at the end of the hall. She alerted me that dinner was served in the dining room only between 7:00 and 8:30. When I asked for a table near the fireplace to take off some of the chill, she laughed. "The lady from Pittsburgh beat you to it by one day. She has requested the same table each evening, but we will get you close to the fire." I thought to myself – "Just the luck, only a handful of people in the hotel and some old pushy retired broad from Pittsburgh has the best table in the house." I was feeling less than charitable tonight after my seven and a half hour drive from the Dublin airport.

I found my room, opened the door, and struggled with my two bags as I entered. My, oh my! The room was just perfect (if first impressions are ever accurate). In the center was a four-poster, canopied bed with a wood-burning stone fireplace diagonally across from the foot of the bed. A comfortable looking, bright red antique wing chair with foot rest sat in the corner where warmth from the fireplace and light from the windows would make for some perfect late-afternoon or evening reading. The room was decorated with enough English chintz to satisfy any woman of breeding – curtains and bedspread matching, but the room still had a bit of a masculine feel. It was a converted hunting lodge after all. The windows, full along the outside wall, were dark walnut mullioned casements that opened out onto a breathtaking garden, wild as all Ireland, but beautiful still as only the English (or in this case Irish) can do. In front of the windows was an antique drop-leaf table and two matching wood armchairs. On the table was a lamp made from an old piece of pottery, some colorful antique glass bottles, and best of all, a pitcher full of fresh cut flowers. Overhead the cream colored ceiling looked as though it had been painted for the last time at least two centuries ago with massive split timbers for support running the length of the room.

Although it was September and cool as I expected by this time, the garden seemed still vibrant with colorful plantings. As I opened one of the casement windows, I was ever so pleasantly assaulted by the late afternoon fragrances of the roses, damp earth, and grass from the garden just below my room. Already I could tell my blood pressure was to be much alieved, and my overall stress...well, it was all but gone. "This is going to be a great getaway" I was beginning to think.

Tired, yet hungry, I unpacked, hanging my sport coats and pants in the handsome old armoire. More than just about anything I wanted a hot bath, maybe a quick shave, and then down to the lobby to get the layout of the lodge, and to the bar to totally unwind before dinner.

The lobby was not really that...more like a living area in a home. Off to one side was the dining room, and to the other side was the bar. As I entered the bar, I was struck again by how pleasing was the decor and layout of the entire place – like a comfortable home instead of a commercial lodging facility. To the right was a long, beautifully crafted wood bar and to the left, a baby grand piano sat surrounded by leather covered stuffed armchairs and two sofas. At the far end of the room was a large bay window, probably 10 feet tall which looked out down the meadow and onto Ballyconneely Bay.

The bartender turned around as I came in, stuck out his hand, and with a broad smile said, "Hi, my name is Mick. Are you Mr. Harte from Texas?"

"Yes, I am. How did you know that?"

"We don't get many folks here from America, let alone Texas" Mick said with a clear curiosity on his face. I ordered my standard Glenmorangie whiskey neat with some water on the side.

"You're a good man Mr. Harte. I knew that as soon as I laid eyes on you."

"Call me Francis. What makes you think that?

"No, it'll be Mr. Harte, if that's okay...Mr. Exall, our owner here, is English and does not permit that first name familiarity with our guests. The reason behind my comment is that my grandfather, Hamish Robertson, worked his whole life in Ross-Shire, Scotland at the very distillery whose whiskey you ordered – Glenmorangie.

It would be too much to fathom to think that you drink his whiskey and were not a good man too, am I right?"

"Okay, Mick, you win – I like your deduction. I am a good man." We had a jovial banter for the next 45 minutes, until Cathleen, Reginald's wife came up to me and suggested my table was prepared in the dining room if I was ready to eat.

"Good-bye for now, Mr. Harte. Your first drink of Glenmorangie is on me," said Mick. "Enjoy your dinner."

As I was walking to my table in the dining room, a real feeling of peace and total, relaxed pleasure was beginning to seep into my bones. Perhaps it was the drink and my tired state after 20 plus hours of travel, but I was feeling very warm and pleased that I had taken Harold's (Dr. Whitson) advice to get away. Cathleen sat me near the roaring fireplace.

The dining room, like everything else about Craggy Rock Lodge had a personality, an ambience that evoked nostalgia for the past, yet was romantic and sophisticated country casual in decor. The table was set with spotless cutlery and stemware on an ironed bright white tablecloth with fresh home grown flowers in a small clear vase. I hoped the food would be a match to everything else I'd experienced so far at the Craggy Rock.

Annie, my cute, freckled waitress asked my preference for dinner between Irish lamb, Scottish beef, or local partridge. I suggested she bring me her favorite, but not overcooked. She winked and said, "You will like what I bring you."

My table location was fine, but I would rather have been in front of the fireplace on this cool night. But, as I recalled, that table had a prior claim by the woman from Pittsburgh. Although others might say I am a controlling individual, I do not ever see myself that way. On this night, nothing was going to spoil my first night's elation at being far, far away from all the stress and problems in Dallas. Those problems somehow would get sorted in my absence, and the Earth would likely continue to turn, no matter what.

As I waited for my first course of she-crab bisque, a woman appeared in the dining room doorway. I am a people watcher when I am away from the office, and this woman was a vision, someone whom I would enjoy watching no matter what she happened to be doing. In her white wool pantsuit and blonde hair, she looked as sexy, yet professional as a woman could look. In the dining room the only other couple, the ones who were celebrating their 50th anniversary this weekend, also looked up to take note of someone about to enter to dine with us. I thought this stunningly beautiful woman could not be the single woman from Pittsburgh who was staying at the Lodge...no, not possible. I earlier this afternoon had already built a mind picture of a retired school marm from Pittsburgh as the woman who had also, like myself, picked the Craggy Rock Lodge for a vacation. But as soon as the thought crossed my mind, she walked into the dining room, over to the table by the fireplace and seated herself. She walked with a gait and erect posture that exuded confidence and grace. We were not ten feet apart at our tables, I and this creature of breathtaking beauty. Wholesome, clean, blue-eyed with high cheek bones, I imagined her to be a model on vacation away from the hustle and bustle of New York. What a surprise, this lady from Pittsburgh!

Before taking the lady's dinner order, Annie asked me if I would like another Glenmorangie and water. That question caused the lady from Pittsburgh to look over and give me a rather strange nod of her head. I wasn't sure what that was about as I tried not to notice. In all truth, I desperately wanted something to cause me to speak to the woman, but decided she might be the type to put a strange man quickly in his place if he tried. I simply said "Yes" to another drink and looked around trying to appear comfortable with myself sitting alone. When you are dining in a room with only three other people in it, and one of them happens to be a polished, beautiful lady alone, it's hard not to take repeated glances her way. By the third time I looked at her, each time having my look returned, I decided this was silly. Why not just break the ice to see if she was interested in talking or not?

"Good evening. My name is Francis," I said as I moved over in her direction. She smiled and asked, "Do you have a last name?" Her approach struck me as a bit unusual, but a genuine smile graced her face, and I thought that to be a good sign. "Harte, Francis Harte," I said. She looked knowingly and asked, "Would Bret be your middle name?" I must have looked stunned as she assumed she was right. "Are you a writer, too, Mr. Francis Bret Harte?"

"You, my dear lady have me at a distinct disadvantage. Two whiskeys on an empty stomach after a tiring day of 20 hours traveling — I am in no condition to match wits with you tonight. However, I am astonished at your acuity. In only two questions, you have ascertained my full name and one of my life's unfulfilled dreams."

"Tell me more," she said with a seemingly genuine interest.

"Okay, but first I have two questions of you." She gave me a go ahead nod. "First," I said, "Are you always in control, and the one giving orders? And second, 'May I join you for dinner?' "

"Why don't you bring over your Glenmorangie and tell me about the first time you ever tasted it," she said with the authority of an admiral or CEO, or even Queen of some empire. I was completely intrigued with this woman! Trying not to look like an enthusiastic schoolboy, I nonetheless quickly retrieved my drink and returned to seat myself opposite this exquisitely tempting Lorelei. Could she be luring me to my doom like the ancient Greek Sirens did to navigators long ago? If there was trouble ahead, I wanted it, so long as she was involved – that was my sense of her at this moment.

Seated, I began, "Yes, I am a frustrated, unfulfilled writer. I am alone, but not lonely. And I forget just where I first tasted Glenmorangie – I think maybe it was in Tunis on my last summer cruise out of Annapolis. Whatever makes you ask such a question, and what do you know of the writer Francis Bret Harte?"

She just looked at me...silently...staring.

"My, but you work fast, Mr. Harte!" It was Annie, the waitress here at the table to take the lady's order.

"I'll have what Mr. Harte is having." she told Annie. "And, pray tell, what might that be?" she said looking even more intently my way.

"You ask a lot of questions! And what is your name or shall I just call you Gladys?"

"You may call me Gladys or Wanda or any old girl-friend you desire, but my name is C.S. Lewis."

"Excuse me?...............................C.S. Lewis? The C.S. Lewis I know from his writings was a famous Oxford professor and man of God. Forgive me, but you do not look like a man of God," I said with a degree of cheeki-ness and a smile.

"Well, it's nice to meet a college man. I'm moderately impressed. You certainly are right, but I am Catherine Schuyler Lewis professionally, but Cathy will be just fine tonight."

"Well Cathy, back to your question of dinner entre...I do not know what I'm having for dinner – just that

Annie promised I would like it, so it looks like we'll both be surprised."

"Do you like surprises?"

"Yes, if they are pleasant," I replied. At that moment Cathy reached across the table, pulled me gently by the yoke of my open shirt toward her and kissed me — not on the cheek, and not platonically. It was a passionate kiss, one that could have been saved for years for the right man returning home after a long sea voyage. I was stunned, and must have looked like a man who's just been hit hard in the face.

Cathy said haltingly, "Oh dear! I think I've scared you away. Forgive me, Mr. Harte?"

I took her hand in mine and, looking intently into her eyes, said, "Cathy, all my life I've wanted to meet a woman where the chemistry was fiery enough and the personality deep enough that it would take an entire lifetime to learn everything. If you have the time, I want to know everything about you! Please start now. Why are you here at this remote hunting lodge tonight? And why all the questions about the whiskey I'm drinking?"

Annie brought Cathy a bottle of white wine and both of us our first course – she-crab bisque soup. "What time do you have to be in bed, Mr. Harte?" Cathy asked with a wink.

"Cathy, I'm in my mid-50's and have all the time that's left to hear your story. So...why are you here tonight and alone?"

"Okay, Bret....I'm going to call you Bret – I'm different than all your other friends. You seem like a genuinely nice man — nice looking, educated, etc. – I, too, would like to get to know you better. I'm a fairly private person, but I will take a risk and answer your questions, and you can judge from there, BUT it will take some time."

Cathy seemed to pull back a bit, hesitated for a full minute or two, and then started her incredible, heart-breaking story. "Bret, two months ago, my life seemed perfect, busy and stressful, but all-in-all, pretty darn good. I was publisher of *Adventure Travel* with a beautiful high up corner office in mid downtown San Francisco, a loving, supportive husband, healthy parents, and most important of all – a gorgeous, unspoiled daughter, Lori, who is on course to graduate with honors from the University of Denver next May. In the space of four weeks, it all came tumbling down."

"My gosh! How? What happened?" I queried, totally interested in what she was telling me.

" *Adventure Travel* was having some serious cash flow problems with a downturn in ad revenues, higher printing costs, and reduced single copy sales as well as subscriptions. We were not in danger of missing our ad guarantee with the Audit Bureau of Circulation, but faced numerous challenges nevertheless. I traveled to Seattle for a conference with key advertising account executives, a trip that had been scheduled for months, long before our problems surfaced. The conference had just started on Thursday, and was to run through the weekend. On Friday night, I received a call from Mom that Dad had suffered a serious stroke that afternoon, and that she needed me in Pittsburgh saying that Dad might not make it!"

"Bret, I tried to contact my husband Richard, but he was not answering his phone at home or work or his mobile number. I just threw my clothes in a bag and headed to SeaTac Airport for the trip home to San Francisco. I planned to continue on to Pittsburgh and have Richard accompany me if he was able, just stopping to get some fresh clothes in the process. All the while I could not reach Richard. When I arrived home, stressed about missing the opportunity to interact with my key ad contacts from all over the U.S. and worried sick about my Dad, I bounded up the stairs and into my bedroom. On that Friday, the 13th, my world came to a cataclysmic abyss, a situation that still racks me physically and emotionally. There in my bed was Richard doing his best 'Oh, my God, you're incredible' routine on top of some nameless vagina. When he looked up and I could see the face of his afternoon conquest – it was Lisa, my best friend for over 14 years. My 'faithful' husband of 29 years whom I had put through law school and my best friend. Bret, I am nothing if not a strong woman. I knew my only significant loyalty right now at this moment was to Mom and Dad and my daughter Lori."

"I walked over to my dresser amidst the gasps, wailing, and 'explanations' and began getting the clean changes of personal items and the clothes I knew I would likely need in case there was a funeral to attend in Pittsburgh. I carried what I needed downstairs, put the items into my bags, and headed out of my home for the last time. I called Lori in Denver and told her that Grandad was likely to pass on in the next few days, and asked if she wished to come with me. Lori loved my Dad. She said yes and could I come through Denver to pick her up at Denver International – that she could be there in three hours? Bret, we flew together to Dad's side at the hospital in Pittsburgh. Poor Dad...he had held on long enough to see Lori and me, and passed peacefully to be with the Lord within half an hour of our arrival. Mom and Lori were devastated; I was so numb as to be almost comatose myself. I knew that I was the only one who could exercise enough strength to get the family through everything that had happened in the last few hours. Of course, Mom and Lori did not know anything about Richard's betrayal."

Annie, the waitress, had hesitated to interrupt us, realizing that some rather heavy conversation was being carried on. She finally asked if we were ready for our entrees. Then she brought out a beautiful rack of Irish lamb in a special sweet berry glaze of some sort – it was awesome and a welcomed break in Cathy's heartbreaking tale of events just a few weeks ago.

I took her hand in mine, and asked, "Can you go on, Cathy?"

She suddenly seemed to think she was boring me with her narrative. "No, not at all, Cathy. This sounds almost like a novel. Please go on."

"Well, Saturday was a long sad day as we made the arrangements for Dad's service and internment. Thankfully, he and Mom had all the major decisions worked out in a pre-need agreement with the funeral home and cemetery. We all decided on a Tuesday memorial service for Dad so that we could get everyone notified and allow for time for the few out-of-town guests to arrive. Of course, the question of when Richard would be arriving came up. On Sunday after church services, I sat Lori and Mom down and said, 'The future of the family belongs to us three women. Richard has violated my trust with another woman. I caught him and her in our bedroom on Friday when I came home unexpectedly, and plan to never talk to him again except in a court of law. Lori, I am so sorry you have to learn this in so difficult and brutal a way. You have lost the two most important men in your life in a short space of time. I wish you to continue a relationship with your father, but he and I are over. And, by the way, the other woman I caught him humping was Lisa, my best friend. You certainly may have whatever conversations you desire with him in the future, and I hope and trust you will. I have set foot in our home for the last time. My new life starts today.' "

"Needless to say, both Mom and Lori were devastated; but we three are strong women. We all are managing to cope slowly with the loss of Dad and with Richard's perfidious behavior."

I remained silent just holding Cathy's hand tightly as we both finished our wonderful lamb entree. I ordered coffee and port for us as we both sat and looked into each other's eyes. "Is there more?" I asked.

"Bret, the bad news was not yet complete. Two weeks after the dust somewhat settled and I returned to work, the board decided to discontinue publication of *Adventure Travel*, putting 280 people out of work including myself. In two months I lost my beloved Father, my husband, and my job. I was angry at God at first, but realized God has blessed me with great parents, education, health, and a wonderful daughter. There are billions of people living and dead who have not been blessed to this degree. I owe God praise and not petty accusations and questions concerning his authority and sovereignty over this world."

"Cathy, why are you here in Connemara, Ireland and why the questions about my drink earlier in the evening?"

"Bret, I've simply run away...away from my responsibilities, my problems, and my debilitating anger over Richard's betrayal of our nearly 30 year marriage. I'm here to see what I can dig up concerning my Father and his early life in County Clare. And Glenmorangie was his drink of choice. Funny, but I've not known any other man who drank it but him until tonight. Dad's favorite writer was born in Albany, New York like my Dad."

"Francis Bret Harte, right?" I asked.

"Yes, he often read to me from his collection of first editions. 'The Luck of Roaring Camp' and 'The Outcasts of Poker Flats' were his favorite two stories."

It had been scarcely three hours since I first met this beautiful, remarkable woman. She was a polished professional, loving Mother and spouse, and tonight a woman in need of careful attention. Our dinner, a wonderful meal, had disappeared in the midst of Cathy's revelations. I had already begun to feel that I wanted desperately to learn more about her. She was the kind of woman with whom cleaning out the garage in our suburban home could be a romantic endeavor – something I had not felt in a long, long time if ever.

The dining room staff was trying to finish their evening and go home. "Cathy, I want to visit with you some more, but tonight, after my 20 hour day of flying and driving, I am just too whipped to be good company any further. Will you have dinner with me tomorrow in town?"

Cathy looked pensive and hesitant for what seemed a long time; finally, she suggested I ask her again at breakfast.

Using a trite old line from college days, I stupidly asked, "Would you want me to call you or nudge you?"

She looked at me unsure as to what to say next. Trying to salvage my reputation (I did not want her to think of me as just another womanizer like her Richard apparently); I apologized and said, "Cathy, I think it's likely neither one of us is that casual in affairs of the heart. Forgive me? I very much want to see you again, and on positive terms that might build something good between us as friends for the long haul. You sound as though you could use an honest male friend, and frankly I, for the first time in a long time, am excited at the prospect of some continued intelligent conversation with a pretty lady."

"Bret, you're not a womanizer. I can sense that about you, and no, I've not taken offense at your question. Yes, Bret, we can get together again tomorrow; I think I'd like that if I, too, can get some sleep tonight."

With that we ended our evening together. She left for her room and I for mine. When I was undressing, waves of good feelings came across me. I had been alone for such a long time, and here was a woman that got my juices flowing as few women before ever have. She was available or so I thought because of her situation and responsiveness to me. Chemistry is such a strange thing – it's hard to manufacture between a man and a woman; it's either there or it isn't.

And with Cathy it definitely was there for me. As tired as I was, it seemed that I might have trouble getting to sleep, so heightened were my feelings – and so unexpected when I started this trip to get away from the stress of business in Dallas.

I undressed completely and slipped between the crisp sheets – oh, what a great feeling, even if it was alone as so many nights before in these last few years. At least tonight, I felt that for the first time in years, I might have someone to care about, a real romance again. It was fun to contemplate. In only moments, I was asleep and soundly.

Dreaming is not something that I do normally. This morning, however, I heard knocking at my door in my sleep. The knocking was soft, but persistent. I awoke wondering what the knocking was about in my dream, but I could still hear the soft knocking – it was at my hotel room door. Why would anyone be trying to reach me at this time of the morning? Looking at my watch, it was close to 2:00 a.m.

When I opened the door in my bath robe, I was stunned to see Cathy standing there in her night clothes.

CHAPTER 2

❧

"**B**ret, would you hold me?"

"Come in," I said as I took Cathy's hand.

"At dinner tonight I realized how much I needed someone to hold me, tell me I'm pretty, and assure me that everything is going to be alright. I've never been a lonely person, but tonight...this morning, I feel so very alone and confused."

I was all but overwhelmed. Nurturing was something I had been very good at doing for my employees and friends, but hadn't the chance to provide it in a romantic way in years. Here was Cathy, trusting in my goodness enough to reach out for what she desperately needed. How little did she realize that my needs matched hers tonight.

With no ritual, we simply disrobed and got into my warm bed together, and I held her close to me. The feel of her hair on my chest, and the smell of her body was the best sensation I've had in years. She had taken off her makeup, yet looked so naturally beautiful that I simply could not believe this was not a dream; that it was a real event happening to me in a place called Ireland.

I awoke to the early first rays of the sun on my first day in Ireland. Lying beside me still sleeping peacefully was Cathy. I simply wanted to savor this feeling. For maybe five minutes I simply stared at this vulnerable creature beside me who trusted me enough to come in the middle of the night to me and ask for exactly what she needed – the warmth of another human to sleep with and protect her at this critical time in her life's journey. Had it only been less than 12 hours since I first laid eyes on Cathy? Is there such a thing as "love at first sight"...for an older, mature man who had all but given up on finding romance again in his life? "My gosh, I hope so," I thought. This seemed real, but still almost too much to comprehend.

I quietly got out of bed and made a pot of coffee while I took my morning shower and shaved for the new day... the first day of the rest of my life! By the time I came out of the shower, the coffee was ready. I took a cup over to Cathy, who was beginning to stir in bed. "Here, you are my dear," I offered. Cathy smiled, took the cup, and sipping its warm strong brew, said, "Bret, this is good, just the way I like it. How did you guess so right?"

"Cathy, I watched you last night...I watched everything you did, including how you took your coffee. I plan to observe you for the rest of your life too. How does that sound?"

"Boldly presumptuous!" as she watched for my reaction. "I think I allowed circumstances to propel me into a much too fast situation with you last night."

"Cathy, I accepted how vulnerable you were...are... and I did not take advantage of the opportunity to become fully intimate last night. Certainly I wanted to, but I felt it might have harmed somehow the beginning of a lifetime romance. What do you really think? Did you not enjoy being in bed with me last night and right now?"

"Oh, Bret, yes! I just am fearful....for the first time in my life I am not sure of anything, and especially my judgment. I cannot believe I knocked on a virtual stranger's hotel room door and asked to come inside and sleep with him. It sounds like something from a trashy novel; I do not live my life in this fashion, and I am fearful I have sent you a terribly wrong message."

"My dear, dear Cathy. Today is the first day of the rest of our lives. What if God has planned for us to spend the rest of our days together? Out of nearly seven billion people in over 140 countries, you and I found ourselves at the same table, in a quaint old hunting lodge, in a small corner of Ireland together last night. That circumstance alone is just too coincidental to have happened without some divine plan having formed it. We are both alone and in need of a real love going forward.

That's what I think! And I want your thoughts after I warm your coffee...just a minute, please."

"Bret, it sounds so enticingly good. I'm just fearful of being emotionally mugged again. Finding happiness is not this easy ever."

"No sweetheart, I do not believe it is easy either."

" 'Sweetheart'? Is that what you think?"

"Yes, I trust that you are exactly who you have described over dinner last evening...that you were a loving, caring spouse and mother, and that you are the innocent, afflicted party in your marriage. And I want to get to know you better and better...how much time do you have?"

"Bret, by how much time, I guess I could say that I have whatever is needed. I am the one who needs to know more about the man I just spent the night with. I need some breakfast. Shall we go down together? The staff is going to be all atwitter at us!"

This is how my Irish getaway began. How could it have happened any better? No, I decided, it just could not be improved, even if I had been writing a novel and could have constructed the scenario any way I desired. What a glorious day this was going to be.

In half an hour, I knocked on Cathy's door; she answered all ready to go. "Wow, am I impressed. I guess when you are just naturally pretty, it does not take long to get ready to go to breakfast."

"Bret, you can knock off the BS. You have my attention for the entire day without all the flattery."

"What I want is your attention for the rest of the month and October too. And by the way, what are you doing for Christmas?"

"Mr. Harte, you are scaring me. I know nothing about you, and I am in no condition to fall in love if there is the least possibility of another sledgehammer blow like the one I have just experienced back at home. 'Home' – I just realized I do not have a home. My God, I'm homeless after half a lifetime of trying to build a home for the three of us. Damn Richard to Hell! Forgive me, Bret? See what you are getting yourself into. I am cool on the outside maybe, but a seething volcano on the inside. Let's go down to breakfast, shall we?"

Coming down the stairs together, Cathleen, the proprietress of Craggy Rock Lodge was waiting to say 'Good Morning'. "I'm glad to see you two have become friends under our roof." Cathy looked up at me, then at Cathleen and said, "Mrs. O'Doyle, something rather special began last night in your dining room. Today, I am determined to find out everything about Mr. Harte. After breakfast you can confide in me what you know about him."

"Mrs. Lewis, the only thing I know is that he is an American gentleman."

"Well, ladies, I must have you both fooled! What's for breakfast, Mrs. O'Doyle?"

"Right this way. We have some fresh blueberries, Belgian waffles, and some just caught trout if you like."

After breakfast while Cathy was finishing her coffee, I sought out Cathleen again to ask her if she could fix a picnic basket that we could take with us on our day of sightseeing up to the Abbey ruins north of town. "Of course, and may I say that I am so pleased you are here to cheer Mrs. Lewis – she's had some most difficult traumas in the last few months, according to her daughter who had arranged this stay for her Mother. Lori will be arriving in a few days to join her Mom."

I looked surprised and Mrs. O'Doyle immediately drew back saying, "Oh, my, I probably should not have told you that fact. It is not my place to reveal our guests' plans. Please do not let on to Mrs. Lewis that I said anything, alright?"

"Yes," I said, "it will be our secret. But thank you for telling me. I am very fond of Cathy already and will look forward to meeting Lori when she arrives."

When I returned to the table, Cathy formed a mischievous smile and said, "I just sent Annie to fish you out of the toilet or bay, whichever one you had fallen into. What are we going to do with this glorious day?"

"Two things I would enjoy with you, Cathy. First I want to go in town and buy you the most beautiful Irish dress we can find, and second, I would like to poke around the old Abbey ruins north of town on the Bay. What say you to my ideas?"

"Bret, whatever is the dress purchase for?"

"Well, Pretty Lady, I want something to remember our first day together. But in secret, I have something else in mind."

"Yes...and what would that be?"

"I want you to look Irish fresh and authentically happy when we see Lori."

She gasped. "How do you know about Lori coming here?"

"I just assumed that before long I might have the chance to meet her somewhere, somehow, sometime. She's coming here?" I asked with a faked surprised look on my face. "What fun that will be!"

"Oh, Bret, whatever am I to do? I cannot just dump your presence in my life on her like that. She is so very distraught at my separation from Richard. For all his faults, Lori is the apple of his eye, and she is much more prone to forgive him than I. She even asked, 'Mom, what did you do to drive Daddy away?' Bret, I do not know if the timing of my meeting you is right for you to be introduced to Lori. I certainly do not wish to give Richard any reason to question my faithfulness or loyalty in court next spring when the divorce proceedings should be finalized."

"Cathy, when is she arriving here in Ireland?"

"I am to pick her up at Shannon Airport on Friday afternoon – that's only two days away. I don't know if I can deal with this just now," she said almost tearfully.

"Cathy, we have two days to figure out a plan, and get to know one another well enough to see if it will still be a problem on Friday. This is all new to me also. I would like to experience our time together hour by hour and savor whatever we can. Someday, I hope this will all be a pleasant part of our collective memories – yours, mine, and Lori's. I hope right now with all my heart that you and I can find enough chemistry and common threads between us to begin building something truly special and permanent, not just a holiday fling. Tell me your thoughts, sweetheart."

"Oh, Bret, you seem too good to be true. You are understanding, and God knows that for me the chemistry is there – 'off the charts' there. I just am scared – scared of a mis-step, scared that I'll be hurt again and irretrievably this time, scared to trust, scared to..."

"Cathy, stop it. Do you not believe in God?"

"Yes, but..."

"Who do you think set our paths to cross? I mean, look around. Here you are, the most beautiful, sensitive person I've ever met, and here am I, someone who desperately wants to love you, care for you, and adore you in all the ways a man can do those things. I've never met a princess before – you're my first!"

"Okay!" Cathy said softly in the cradle of my arm.

"What does 'Okay' mean?" I asked.

"It means you've got me totally for the next two days with this warning. If you turn out to be a rat in a prince's outfit, I'll kill you in the most painful way possible. Do you want to proceed?"

"My, but you are direct," I said as I kissed her. "I want to explore every part of your body, your mind, your history, and I've maybe got only 30 or 40 years to finish. Let's get started!"

"With my body?"

I smiled and said, "Yes, tonight, if you are not too tired from shopping and rock climbing around the Abbey! When is your birthday?"

"That's a curious question. It's the same as the Queen's."

"Her real birthday or the day it's celebrated?"

"The real day."

"So I'll be taking you out on April 21st, right?"

"You are persistent and presumptuous, Bret Harte. Well, maybe so," Cathy said.

"Now, I should know yours. When is your birthday?"

"Tonight,"

Cathy gave me a look I'll always remember. "If that's truly the case, then I have a gift for you that you'll never forget, Bret."

I pulled her to me again and held her face just inches from mine, "Cathy, I will desire you always and all ways for so long as I live – that much I know already, right now, right here above Ballyconnelly Bay. Get ready.... ready for a grand ride, girl!" I said as I kissed her and pulled her slim body against mine.

"It feels like you might be ready now," Cathy said as she touched me below the belt.

"You are right." You make me feel like a teenage boy, and that's a great thing for a man my age. Let's get to town to find you a dress. I promise the passion will still be there tonight."

"Tonight?" she asked disappointedly.

"Cathy, you are in complete control of me right now. I care deeply for you and whatever you want, I want."

"I want the smell of you on me when I try on my new dress later today. Meet me in my room in fifteen minutes and let's unwrap your birthday gift?"

"Is that a suggestion or an order," I asked smugly.

"It's your birthday, but you're down to 14 minutes. Why don't you get a move on?"

When she opened the door to her room, Cathy was wearing only a bath towel with a "Do Not Disturb" door hanger in her hand. The next hour was something straight from a sexual "how to" book. She was ravenous and unquenchable, no less than I was after more than four years of self-imposed celibacy. After repeated lovemaking, I looked her in the eye and said, "Cathy, if you never believe anything again in this world, believe that I have fallen irretrievably in love with you, and no one and nothing can ever interfere with that feeling."

"Bret, you say all the things I want desperately to hear. Thank you for being so tender and thoughtful in your lovemaking. We have begun on a special journey. I am excited again about life and going into the future. Happy Birthday, Darling!"

"Let's get you that dress I promised. You can wear it when you next see Richard and tell him a special guy bought it for you in Ireland. Is he the jealous type?"

"Bret, there need never be any secrets between us, but right now I do not want Richard's name or thoughts of him and his perfidy to enter this beautiful picture we are painting. Is that okay with you? I will tell you he will be livid at the thought of someone entering 'his' domain. I was his property and not a whole lot else. Done with talk of Richard, alright?"

Reginald Exall was at the front desk when we started to leave for town. I asked him if he knew of a good ladies wear retailer, a dress shop in town. He said, "Just a moment... Cathleen will have a great resource for you. Her sister runs the best little boutique this side of the Atlantic."

"Cathleen," he called out, " Can you direct Mr. Harte and Mrs. Lewis to Lenore's shop?"

"Your timing is perfect, Mr. Harte," Cathleen said as she appeared from around the corner with a lovely old fashioned wicker picnic basket in hand. I just finished your basket; be careful with the silver utensils, they were my Grandmother's."

Cathy was surprised. "Silver utensils? We are so used to plastic in the States. Cathleen, I like your trust and sense of style. Thank you. We'll bring it all back except the food," I said with a laugh. Cathy looked at me and asked when I decided to have a picnic for two and where. I told her that Mick, the bartender had suggested a great location for a picnic and suggested that I ask you before he did. "You've caused quite a stir in only a few days here."

"Do I look that available and needy?"

"No, Sweetheart, but we guys need to practice to see if we still have what it takes to get a woman's attention, and you're the only game at the Inn, ha!"

"Flattered or offended...I'm not sure what the proper response should be, Bret."

"Probably a little bit of both, Cathy. I'll go around to the side and get the car so we can be off on our shopping and exploring excursion."

We drove into town, a rather quaint seaside village, and found 'Lenore's On High', Cathleen's sister's dress shop/boutique on High Street. I am not normally a shopper; in fact, the last thing I would ever do on a European getaway is spend time in a dress shop. But just being with Cathy and watching her enjoy herself was an elixir for me now that I had totally fallen under this woman's spell. She obviously was having a great time being the center of attention as she tried on dress after dress for me to view, asking each time the typical female questions of "Does this one make me look fat? What do you think of this color on me etc., etc.?" At last we agreed on two dresses that were best on her; she could not decide which, so I suggested we just take both of them. The total price for both was not steep, but Cathy made such a fuss as if it was at Parisian designer prices. Clearly she was happy; something that probably hadn't happened in weeks since all the traumatic events had first begun to unfold. Seeing her smile and feeling good about being with me was worth ten times the price of the dresses. Wrapping them both – one a form fitting white dress with narrow straps and small Irish four-leafed clovers on those straps was my favorite. The other was a green sundress with Irish wildflowers randomly placed on the fabric, and it, too, looked good on her.

Now it was time to explore the ruins of the 9th
century abbey on the outskirts of town. We had a
grand time scampering over the tumbled down walls
like a couple of children, clearly having more fun
than two professional desk bound executives had a
right to expect. Mick's private picnic spot was not
hard to find. After spreading the blanket amid the
remaining wildflowers on the high hillside overlooking the ocean, we began an afternoon's outing that
would carry memories for years afterward. We talked
of everything and nothing. Cathy was determined to
get to know me. She asked questions about my marriage and children.

"Cathy," I said, "my marriage was never a good one. I
married late —30 years-old – for the sake of having children more than for love. Cathy, I was a bit of a pompous
ass when I married, not totally in love, but proceeding
anyway for fear of losing a pretty good lady...her name
was Ellen, and we had been dating for two years. I was
working for The New York Times and on my way to my
first million dollars or so I thought. A funny thing happened around the midpoint of our marriage. As I began
to fall in love with her, she was falling out of love with
me. I'll never forget the day of our tenth wedding anniversary; I flew in early on Thursday from a business trip
to Philadelphia to take her to an elegant restaurant to
celebrate our special day/evening. When I came bounc-
ing into the house, my shock was similar to yours with
Richard except Ellen was not there. Cathy, our Dallas
house was empty! I was angry that burglars had cleared
us out and immediately called the police. I'll also never
forget my conversation with the desk sergeant on duty.

When I asked him to send over a detective so I could file a report, he asked me what was missing. 'Everything', I said. He asked me if I was in the house and what I was looking at. I was beginning to get a little annoyed and told him, 'Look, I told you already that everything is missing – there's a few books and clothes stacked in the corner.'

He asked me if I was having marital troubles. 'No, no more than any couple,' I said. The officer suggested that I sit down for a few minutes and call him back if I truly believed that I was the victim of a burglary. Here's the funny part; his next statement was, 'Mr. Harte, thieves don't stack shit!' It was only then that the enormity of what was actually going on hit me fully. It's been 18 years ago, and I still have some residual hurt when I think back to that afternoon."

"Oh, Bret, I am so very sorry. No one deserves to be dealt so harsh a blow without cause. It sounds like we both are damaged goods to some extent. But you seem to have no bitterness in you over Ellen's betrayal of her vows to you."

"Cathy, it's been a long time ago, almost 20 years, in my case – not fresh like yours. I've had adequate space and counseling to heal almost all of the old wounds. I kid people who ask about my ex by telling them she was a man hater. She wrote a book called *Men Are Pigs and Deserve to Die.* That title did not sell, so she joined with Louis Farrakhan and wrote a second edition called *White Men Are Pigs And Deserve To Die,* that one I think sold eight copies."

Because of the smile I had on my face, Cathy looked quizzically at me and said, "You're joking, Bret, right?" After a few seconds, she knew she was right, and laughed.

"It's good to see you smile and laugh. You're going to make it through this period of temporary difficulties and become more productive and happy than you've ever been before. Of this I am confident. I only hope to be along for the ride as you re-blossom in this new life of yours."

"Bret, I am happy at this moment, but somewhere out there," she pointed westward out over the Atlantic, "are some million bedeviling details that are not going to be pleasant as I fight for resolution of them all. Are you sure you are up to the fight with me? And what about your own life in Dallas and your business?"

"Cathy, finding the love of a lifetime is worth whatever barricades have to be smashed and raging rivers that have to be forded. Let me worry about the Bret issues; you just focus on how I can help. Some days it may be just getting out of the way, and other days just holding you and listening. If we can be together at the end, then it will all have been worth it."

"I cannot believe the serendipity of these last 72 hours – how I picked this time, Ireland, and this particular lodge, the Craggy Rock all meshing with your schedule – it's just incredible! I mean, a few days different, 50 miles different and we likely would have never met."

"Well, it kind of reinforces my notion that God is in charge and has a plan for my life as well as yours, don't you think, Cathy?"

"Yes, I guess you are right, and God knows how I like new dresses, ha! Bret, it looks like rain is coming. Shouldn't we pack up and return to the car?"

"Cathy, how many times have you walked in a soft Irish rain? Well, me neither. If we get wet, we'll also get dry, and have the memory of this beautiful day always. Give me a moment. I'm going to set my camera on a tripod and take a photo for our first album, okay?"

Cathy was right. The rain came and it was not so soft, but rather a downpour, but not too cold on our unprotected bodies – neither of us had brought a coat or an umbrella. There was an abandoned shed not too far away, and we made a dash for it. Inside, I pulled Cathy to me and kissed her as the waves of passion began to flow. Was it always going to be like this in her presence? She did not hold back, but pressed her wet, warm, slim frame against mine. We spread the picnic blanket a second time, but this time for a feast of a different sort. Cathy was insatiable in her appetite for sex. I think I understood why, with no one to give outlet to her desires for several months, I guessed. "Cathy, you are an incredible lover. Richard must be out of his mind to let you go."

"Bret, Richard was a lousy lover, short on equipment and knowledge as to how to best use it. He thought of himself as a ladies' man, always flirting in social settings, only I did not suspect he was actually consummating any of his flirtations. You, my friend, have awakened a woman to an extent that you may come to regret. I want you, and fear that I may need you more than you can withstand."

"We shall see. I think you are wrong in this one concern, but you can continue to pass your ratings on to me if you like, and I will always try to please you. You know that, don't you?"

"Bret, I am so comfortable right now, and that scares me a little bit. What happens when we come to the end of this short overseas vacation?"

"Sweetheart, that is a genuine concern, and I think we should talk about it tonight or tomorrow. It's been a long, but beautiful day – the best birthday I can remember since my fifth birthday, and that was a while ago. Let's go back to the lodge and have a quiet meal at your table by the fire, shall we?"

"Yes, let's do just that. Do you think Cathleen, Reggie, and the staff will think we've been making love all over the Irish countryside?"

"They might have their suspicions. I think we are good for their business; love and new relationships make the whole world go 'round. Mick and little Annie might be jealous. Our story will be told for months after we've left. Frankly, I'm already thinking about a return someday soon."

"Oh, my gosh, Bret. Are you always thinking so far ahead? I'm just praying for the next 90 days to pass with only a few major catastrophes. At dinner tonight, I'd like to discuss Lori and whatever I am to do about her feelings in all this kettle of fish."

We brushed the straw and debris from off the blanket, wrapped it around us both, and started for the car, the rain still falling, but not so hard as before. "What'll we call the little shed or barn? I want to remember it, this day, and how incredible you were," Cathy said.

As we got inside the car and began our drive back to the Craggy Rock, I said, "How about 'Beginish'? There's a little island in Dingle Bay called 'Beginish'; I think we began something very special this afternoon in that little barn."

" 'Beginish' it is. If you're ever bored at a party and I am there with you, just whisper 'Beginish' in my ear, and I will beat you outside, ha! Deal?"

"You've got it...my promise....if I ever hear you say 'Beginish', we stop whatever it is we're doing, and head for the nearest place we can be alone."

"Even if we're fighting?"

"Especially if we're fighting!" I exclaimed. "But are we ever going to do that? Fight, I mean."

"My dear man, if you've not noticed yet, men and women are wired vastly different. You may think you love me now, but give it some time. When your lust wears thin, you'll find some things about me, not too many, I hope, but some things that just irritate the hell out of you. So, yes we will have conflict, but I hope you remember your new word, 'Beginish'. Promise?"

"Yes. Here we are. How long do you need in your room to get ready for dinner?"

"Bret, darling, can you give me an hour or so?"

"I'll see you in the bar around 7:30 this evening." What a day this had been. Is it possible to feel this strongly about a woman, I've only known for literally a few hours? I guess one of the great things about having lived for over 50 years is that you come to terms with yourself. At this time of my life, I had become comfortable with and accepting of me. I knew my strengths and my weaknesses, my gifts and my shortcomings, and just was not concerned about what anyone thought....except Cathy...from now on.

After taking a hot shower and shaving some of the stubble from my face, I felt a lot better....rested and at peace with everything. Yes, I was excited as almost never before, but not stressed like just a few days ago when I was submerged in the cauldron of work at my Dallas company. I went down to the bar and began recounting the day's adventures to Mick, the bartender. At 7:30 sharp, Cathy walked into the bar, and caught every eye in the place. She looked absolutely stunning, more beautiful than any runway model half her age. She was wearing a dark, form fitting pantsuit with a blue-striped open collar blouse. With her blonde hair just touching the collar of the suit and her décolletage just barely meeting the proper decorum, she was my vision, probably every middle-aged man's vision of an ideal date.

I rose to meet her and give her a chilled glass of Sauvignon Blanc that I had Mick to pour at 7:30. As Cathy kissed me on the cheek, I whispered in her ear, "Sweetheart, I'm not sure I'll make it through dinner sitting across from you without virtually committing an act that likely will get us thrown out of the place."

"Cathy laughed and said, "Virtually? I can do without the vichyoisse tonight...and the cabbage and corned beef!"

"Forgive me, sweetheart. I'll control myself for now, but you do look captivating. Let's go to dinner and spend some time talking about the immediate future ...and long-term too if you like."

The dining room was busier tonight. The party of German tourists had taken six or seven tables and there was the older couple celebrating their 50th anniversary weekend. Looking at the older couple, I couldn't help wondering how Cathy and I might look if we made it to some anniversary milestone together. Cathy noticed too and said, "Look at that older couple. Don't they look good together? I mean 'in love' still after all these years?"

"Cathy, you've got to quit that!"

"What?" she asked with a bit of alarm in her voice.

"Reading my mind," I said with a smile on my face. After we had been seated and ordered our meal for the evening, I said to this incredible woman sitting across from me, "Cathy, I have fallen in love with you totally. I know it sounds preposterous on the surface, but I also know that you are not a woman to engage in casual affairs. After having made love several times in a short span, I want to get your feelings...explicitly."

"Bret, it's true that I, too, am totally absorbed. It all has happened so fast that I simply have not taken it all in, not processed it, not thought ahead as to however we might make a long-term commitment work with me living in San Francisco and you owning a business in Dallas. A Texan, for God's sake...have I lost my mind?" she said with a smile in her voice.

"Of two things you can be certain. One, I love you with all my heart for all time. Two, it is going to work out. I too haven't figured out all the details, but it is going to happen – we are going to be together."

"Bret, you do not know my family, and Lori doesn't have a clue about you. She's still hoping that I will come to my senses and take Richard back. It seems so strange to contemplate my life as a single woman that I must admit until last evening, I was thinking of giving in to Lori's wishes and allowing Richard to grovel his way back into my life."

"And now?"

"Oh, Bret, I don't know. It seems so right on one hand, but so scary in all its uncertainties on the other."

"Cathy, you do not have to do anything right now. I would like to ask you to allow me time with you for you to gradually become more and more comfortable with the idea of an 'us' for the long haul. There are no skeletons or ghosts in my closets to someday haunt you. In time you will come to realize how very similar we are, and how good we will be together. See the old couple to your right...50 years together... that could be us someday... at least maybe 25 years together, since we did not meet in college."

"Bret, you say all the right things, do all the right things. I would be foolish not to seriously consider what you are suggesting, darling. Can you be patient with me? There's so much on my plate coming up in the next six months, I am scared out of my wits to think of making a mistake right now by being overly hasty."

"Does that mean you want to sleep alone tonight?" I asked with a gleam in my eye.

"No, Bret, you have opened Pandora's box. I'll never want to sleep alone in Ireland."

"I understand. It's San Francisco I'm worried about."

"Would you like to come out west to see me?"

"Sure, where are you living there?"

"Damn it all! I suppose I will have to take an apartment or a condo until the marriage...I mean the divorce is settled. It all sounds so strange after 30 years living with one man. My life will never be the same. I will be a stranger in my own house as I go back to collect my things."

I took her hands in mine. "My darling, life is going to be wonderfully different for both of us. Somehow I will be there to support you and protect you from any crass behavior or legal attacks from Richard. We only need to be careful not to give him any ammunition for grounds to make you culpable for his deceit."

"You are so right! I am glad you understand how careful I must be. If an account of my behavior here with you ever reached him, he would make a big thing legally out of it. Richard, for all his faults, is not a dumb lawyer. Together we have accumulated a sizeable estate, and that's property and money I will need, at least my half of it."

"Cathy, we have some time to work out a plan for you, for us. Tonight, let's ask the English couple to join us for a nightcap in the bar in their honor, what do you say?"

"Yes, that would be something nice to take the focus off ourselves. Are you always this considerate?"

We decided to have our coffee in the bar. On the way out of the dining room, Cathy and I went over to the other couple's table. I introduced Cathy and myself to them; they were the Randolph's, Scott and Evelyn Randolph. "Why yes, Evelyn and I would enjoy joining you in the bar. Why don't you and your lady get a place beside the piano; we'll be there shortly," said Mr. Randolph.

Within a few minutes, Mr. and Mrs. Randolph entered the bar with Evelyn seating herself at the baby grand piano as Scott took his place beside her in an overstuffed wing chair. What began next was an act worthy of any Las Vegas lounge – Evelyn vigorously playing the piano as it likely had never been played before while Scott played the 'bones'. Cathy was enthralled, having never seen so unique a duo perform. When Evelyn played the "Yellow Rose of Texas", she totally won me over, if she had not before then. We ordered two rounds of after dinner drinks which was a cheap price to pay for such a grand show. Finally around 11:30, Mrs. Randolph closed the piano cover and rose to her feet. "Oh, please do not stop," I protested.

"I'm sorry, Mr. Harte," she said, "but Scotty and I have an appointment upstairs" as she kissed Scott and winked our way.

Cathy melted. "That's exactly what I want!" as she took my arm.

"Well, I'll learn the bones if you can master the baby grand."

"No, silly, I'm talking about their obvious love for each other after all these years. That's so romantic, it brings a tear to my eye!"

I looked longingly into Cathy's eyes. "Your room or mine?" I whispered in Cathy's ear.

"Mine, in five minutes."

"I'll give you two!"

"Okay, if you insist. Set your clock" Cathy said with a laugh.

CHAPTER 3

⌘

We awoke to a bright, sunny autumn morning amidst the reality of what Ireland is famous for – 40 shades of green.

"We need to talk; Lori is landing this afternoon at Shannon Airport. She's not aware that I would be anything but alone on this trip; it was my plan to just be alone, contemplate, plan my next moves, and find some time to explore my Dad's heritage here in County Clare, the latter in the company of Lori."

"Cathy, we've made a permanent connection, but I am completely sensitive to your position with regards to Lori and will behave as you wish." That was particularly hard for me to say; I wanted to know everything and become a part of everything she was, is now, and will be in the future. Was I being unrealistic? Patience, I told myself.

"Bret, I know you want to accompany me to Shannon, but Lori thinks she is coming to help me come to terms with seeing her Daddy and putting our lives back the way it used to be before Richard's infidelity. I am not sure how best to handle this mess, but I cannot introduce you just now. Give me some time alone with Lori? Please..."

"Anything you wish, sweetheart. I'm cognizant that it will take some time, but I'll be crazy if it takes too long to get back to having my arms around you... on a regular basis. I know I cannot stay here at the Craggy Rock Lodge and see you in the public spaces and stay away from you. Perhaps it's best for me to leave and for us to plan to get together soon in the states. You could stop off in Dallas or I could join you in San Francisco after you return home. In fact, here's the plan that makes the most sense to me...you fly to Dallas and join me for a few days as a break in your journey home. I'll fly to San Francisco with you after that. Do you know where you'll be living for the immediate future?"

"Oh, Bret, I don't know. There's so much I need to do, to think about. I must put together a plan for the immediate future, find a new job, and then begin to think about the long-term."

"My darling, I do not know how everything is going to work. I only know this for certain – that you and I are going to be together for whatever time God gives us on this Earth, and that two heads are better than one. We'll take one day at a time, and when you are finally free of Richard, we'll be married and honey-moon any place you wish, although I hope it is back here in Ireland."

"Bret, I wish I could be as calm and certain of the future as you are, but I just can't right now."

"Cathy, my darling, enjoy your time with Lori, and return with her as far as Dallas. She can continue on to Denver, and then you and I can spend some time alone in Texas and put a plan in place for you when you arrive back in the Bay area. I'll take you down to my favorite B&B in the Hill Country and we will commit a plan to paper, I promise."

"Is that all?"

"No, my darling, there'll be lots of long walks, romance, hand holding, kissing, and unlimited, uncon-ditional love-making."

"Bret, you make it all sound so easy, and it is easy when I am with you, away from every care I have, but a day of reckoning has to be forthcoming."

"Sweetheart, I will be there for you always. Say you'll see me in a few days in Texas?"

"Whatever am I going to tell Lori about you, about us?"

"I do not see that as any particular issue that has to addressed at this stage. If my name comes up, I can be someone who is helping you with your high level job search. Now we'll need to be heading to Shannon soon. I'll leave you the car and board my flight to Dallas just as you meet Lori. I'm going to get online and see what flight I might still get for this afternoon."

"You seem to have everything worked out in your own mind, Bret. I hope life's reality is as easy to traverse as you think."

"One step at a time my dear, dear Cathy. I'm hoping you'll agree to my next step."

"Which is...?"

"Making love to you for the last time in Ireland," I said longingly.

"Yes," was the reply as she fell back into bed on top of me.

CHAPTER 4

Sometimes, serendipity has a way of working everything out – I was able to land a seat on the last
flight today back to the U.S. with a stop in Boston
and on to DFW later tonight. It took off from Shannon
around three hours after Lori was scheduled to land.
Maybe I could stand in the wings and watch as Cathy
met her daughter, and still make my departure a few
minutes later – it was worth a try. When I explained my
plan to Cathy, she amazed me by remaining calm and
agreeing to it. It would, after all, be a neat thing to see
this young woman, who likely was going to become my
step-daughter. No, I thought – not step-daughter, just
daughter as if she were my own. She was part of Cathy,
and, as a consequence, to be part of me in the future.
I was still finding it hard to believe that this love I had
found here in Ireland was so real, so deep, and so permanent – all in so short a space of time. It was only four
days ago I saw Cathy for the first time in my life. Oh, I
had envisioned her many times over the last years, but,
until now, she had never materialized. "Life just contin-

ues to educate you" was a saying of my father, and how little did I appreciate it until now.

I packed my bags, carried them down to the car, and loaded them before making my rounds to say good-bye to the staff at Craggy Rock Lodge – they all had been wonderfully attentive.

Mick said, "It's been a short visit, but a good one, right?" as he winked at me.

"One of the very best ever, Mick. I hope to see you again. When are you coming to the states?"

"I have to work 50 weeks a year here in Ireland to keep the creditors at bay, Mr. Hart. One of these days I'm going to take a month off and come to America."

"Great, Mick. I'll be expecting a call when you land in Dallas."

"At that moment, Mrs. O'Doyle came by the bar and said, "I hope you've enjoyed your stay, Mr. Harte. Reggie and I hope you will come back."

"I think you can count on that happening, Cathleen. It has been a life changing stay....meeting Mrs. Lewis and all. In fact she's taking me to Shannon Airport in a few minutes for my trip back to Texas. While we are on the way to Shannon, could you arrange to have some fresh cut flowers put in her room along with this note? Here's 50 Euros; will that cover it?"

"Yes, Mr. Harte, I'll be able to do that." We don't know the entire story, but it sounds like a romantic one with a good ending, I hope! And there'll be no charge. Consider it my contribution to a blossoming romance that started at Craggy Rock Lodge."

"Cathleen, you're the best hostess ever!"

Cathy came down the staircase and walked over to where the two of us were talking, and putting her arm in mine, said, "Ready?"

Cathleen said, "I'll be meeting Lori, your daughter later today, right, Mrs. Lewis?"

"That's the plan, but first I've got to get this handsome man to his plane bound for Texas."

"You need to be off then. See you, Mrs. Lewis, when you return. And Mr. Harte, good luck with your plans," Cathleen said as she winked at me.

In the car on the way to the highway (more like a Texas Farm-To-Market Road), I asked Cathy to tell me how she would like things to go at Shannon Airport when we met Lori.

"You CANNOT be revealed as the new love of my life...Lori could never handle the shock of that. I'm thinking a bit of white-lie telling will have to take place, if you are to meet her. Lori is very close to her dad; Richard spoiled her completely over the years. I have been forced into the role of disciplinarian and am loved less because of that role. But she is my only child, and I love her with all the love that any mother can have for someone to whom she gave birth. Oh, Bret, I am rambling so. I know you want to meet Lori, but what in the world do I tell her? Who are you, Bret?"

"Cathy, you are beautiful. Have I told you that today? How's this for an explanation? I am an American investor who is soon launching a new magazine by the name of *Forty Shades of Green*, a title that will carry articles about the culture, history, geography, and future of Ireland. I've been here for the last month setting up temporary office space for the new publication. One of my goals is to obtain an experienced editor-in-chief who can help me pull the project off and draw tourists to Ireland. Today was a second interview with you that we arranged to be held at Shannon Airport because of Lori's arrival later in the day. I bent my schedule to accommodate yours because I want you badly as my editor (and life partner, but we'll not broach that just yet, right?)."

"Oh, Bret, that's brilliant. It sounds so good that I want to believe it myself. Yes, that's our story. Pull over, Bret. Do you think we have time to.....?"

"Cathy, forget it! What am I going to do with you? I think I have finally met my match – someone whose libido matches my own...maybe even stretches a little beyond mine. Cathy, listen to me for a minute. There is nothing, Darling, that you could ever do to make me stop loving you. Do you hear me?"

"Bret, I don't want you to go back to Texas without me, but I promised Lori we would have some time alone together to put a plan in place for the future. I also promised her we would explore her grandfather's roots in County Clare. I am really looking forward to Lori's ideas and helpful input as I go forward in my life without a man beside me," she said as she winked at me. She noticed we were already at Shannon. "My, that seemed a quick trip, Bret. Once Lori gets through customs, I'll introduce you as Mr. Harte who has been discussing my coming to work for the new magazine. You can invite us both to lunch with you here at the airport before you depart for the U.S. this afternoon. It should go perfect except for the part where I see you off with a handshake at the departure lounge. Help me stay strong at that point, okay?"

Cathy and I entered the terminal building and took up a position near where people from Lori's flight from New York City would be passing out once customs was cleared. I looked at Cathy and asked her if she was nervous in any way or just excited at the prospect of spending time with Lori without any distractions to mar the week. "Bret, I am okay except I am already missing you and dreading the crap I need to sort through in putting together a new life. Lori will claim to be neutral, but in reality she will be an advocate for Richard, so the week will be difficult instead of a fun journey through Irish family history."

The next fifteen minutes were surreal. I could not have dreamed a scenario like what was about to unfold. As the portal from customs began to spew forth the mostly American passengers who had arrived from New York City and other points before New York, I watched as Cathy's face turned ashen. "Oh, no!.... No!.....Shit!"

"Darling, what's the matter?" I was becoming alarmed by Cathy's distress.

"The blonde in the red dress is Lori. See the man behind her with the slicked, silver hair?...that's Richard... Richard Lewis....my profligate, philandering soon to be former spouse. He must have conned her into coming along and 'fixing' everything!"

"Bret, I do not want to talk to him. Thirty years of marriage and the only image I can see is him humping my best friend in our bed in my house! ....I'm furious... Bret, get me out of here!"

"Darling, I will. First, for civility's sake, you have to say hello to Lori, tell her of your dismay, mind your tongue just for a few minutes, and then I can talk for you if you are too over-the-top to go forward. I'm here and will do anything you need, okay?"

Lori caught a glimpse of her mom and came running over to Cathy, shrieking all the way. I felt sorry for poor Lori – she was so happy to see her mom and was probably anticipating that her angelic presence and diplomatic skills could make everything right again. Unfortunately for Lori, Cathy (and I) had embarked on a journey which would forever leave behind that only life that Lori had ever known.

"Mom, are you glad to see me?"

"Lori, I love you and am always glad to see you. But I am afraid you have mis-judged badly by allowing your dad to intrude into our time...it was to be just you and me for some badly needed R&R together."

"Oh, Mom, please just listen for a minute...Daddy is hurting; he's so sorry for everything."

"Lori, I do not expect you to understand anything of what Richard has caused by his over-the-top rutting behavior with Lisa. I do not want to see him, I do not want to talk to him, I do not want to hear his voice, and I will not soon forgive and forget your bringing him here."

By this time, Richard had come up to join the two women in his life, not quite realizing the depth and volume of anger his unannounced arrival had precipitated. Cathy spun on her heels and walked away toward the lobby doors. I ran after her to suggest that I talk to the two new arrivals, explain who I was according to our earlier discussion, and then return to take her wherever she wished to go. "Give me a few minutes alone with them, Cathy...okay? I love you and we will get through this day."   .

With that I went back to a bewildered Lori and her father and introduced myself, first to Mr. Lewis and then to Lori. "Pardon me for an inadvertent intrusion on personal family matters. Mrs. Lewis asked me to intercede on her behalf until she can better process whatever it is that's going on right now between the three of you. I am Francis Harte, a stateside investor. My plans for a new Irish magazine require an experienced editor. My second interview with Mrs. Lewis was scheduled here at Shannon Airport this morning so she could meet you afterwards upon your arrival, Lori. If you will be so kind as to give me your hotel or a way to contact you, I will pass it on to Mrs. Lewis. She is not feeling well and I will be escorting her back to her hotel."

"Now just a minute... Mr. Hark, is it?" Richard Lewis interjected.

"Harte, Francis Harte." I was surprising myself how calm I was in the face of this man whom I should be despising for what he had done to Cathy. The fact was I was feeling a bit of sympathy for him for what he could not possibly know of Cathy's current and probably permanent state of mind.

"Cathy is my wife. Lori and I have flown all night to see her. You are right; this is an intrusion, an unwanted one just now on your part. I insist you take us to wherever you have removed Cathy, and then leave us." He was getting pretty fired up. For an attorney to get so volatile and rude so quickly took me aback, but this was about his property rights in his mind I supposed.

"I'm sorry, but I have my instructions from Mrs. Lewis which I feel obliged to honor. Here is my local telephone number. If you have any messages for Mrs. Lewis, I'll be sure she gets them promptly if you call. Lori, it was good to meet you; I only wish it was on more pleasant terms. Good day." With that I went to the car where Cathy was waiting.

"Bret, how much time do we have before your flight?"

"Approximately three hours.....why?" I wasn't sure what was coming with all the angst of the moment.

"Do you think there's time for me to get on your flight?"

I hesitated in my answer.

"Well, do you?"

"Cathy, it would be close, but I think we might be able to accomplish it. What exactly are you thinking, Darling?"

"Bret, please take me out of here. I do not want to be anywhere Richard can find me. I do not want to talk to him, or listen to his arguments, his whining, his demands.....nothing to do with him...period!"

"Okay, Sweetheart, but what about Lori? She'll be hurt, won't she?"

"Bret, let's move! Yes, my poor Lori will be hurt, but she brought this on by allowing Richard to know of my plans. She cannot know the depth of my heartache; she just opened the wound that had started to heal. Bret, Honey, I am not so callous as I appear, but I just want out of here tonight, so I can wake up with you in Texas or New York....anywhere that Richard isn't. Okay?"

"Okay, Cathy," I said as I turned onto the road leading away from Shannon and toward Craggy Rock Lodge. "To pull this off, we are going to have to operate like a military team. I'm taking command right now. Here's what you need to do. Call American Airlines – the number locally is number 3 on my phone. Tell the agent that you want to get on my exact itinerary with a seat to accompany me. My advantage number is NB37667. I can talk to them if required. Do that now so we can be finished by the time we pull up to Craggy Rock Lodge, okay?"

Cathy did not argue; she just did as I asked. I was liking this woman more and more. She was asking something of me, and did as I asked to get her own desire filled. We (she and I) were going to continue to get along, I was sure of it. I have always liked strong, willful women. I am the same kind of man, and usually have huge arguments with the women I am attracted to.

"Here's my credit card if they need it, Cathy,"

"Oh, Bret, you truly are wonderful, but I will use mine. I do not expect you to pay for my madness....not yet anyway, ha!"

During the next fifteen minutes, Cathy was able to accomplish the change in the plane ticket from her original itinerary to mine. "Bret, it's done! I am so excited. Do you know that other than changing planes,

I've never been to Texas? Now, are you sure of what you're getting yourself into?"

"Cathy, the more important question is, are you prepared to meet my Mother?"

"Wow, you are serious...I think you like me!"

I could do nothing other than stop the car on the shoulder of the tiny roadway, get out, and go over to her side of the car. I asked her to open the door. When she did, I dropped to my knees and said simply, "Cathy, will you marry me?"

She started laughing uncontrollably, and then, when she saw how crestfallen and confused I looked, she stopped...silence....she started to cry. "Oh, Honey, the answer is YES, if you can give me some time...I mean I am not even divorced yet!"

I jumped back into the car. "Good, we might make it to Dallas tomorrow after all."

As we continued the drive toward Craggy Rock Lodge, Cathy looked my way and said, "You are really something, you know that? You never cease to surprise me. Are you sure about your question?"

"Cathy, all my life I've wanted to find someone like you with whom to share whatever years I have left on this earth. I've looked and looked, and spent many an hour in the presence of women who, although nice for the most part, were simply not the one. Darling, there is no one like you – of that I am convinced. We have both been hurt terribly. I can imagine nothing better nor more satisfying than to heal together over the years. Yes, Dear, I am sure. Right now I cannot imagine spending my life without you – YOU, nobody ever but you."

We pulled into the lane that led to Craggy Rock. "Remember", I said, "we are on a tight time schedule. Cathleen was watering her flower garden near the front door and looked up, quite surprised to see both of us here.

"Oh, Mr. Harte, please tell me you didn't miss your plane."

"Right, Cathleen. Cathy, while you begin packing, I'll fill Mrs. O'Doyle in as to what's going on."

In ten minutes I entered Cathy's room and was surprised to see her almost fully packed. Cathy came over to me just dancing like a teenage girl. She grabbed me hard around the neck and said, "You did not know you would be coming back to the lodge today, maybe ever. There are these beautiful flowers here along with this note. I love this room where some glorious moments of passion have unfolded for me. Is it alright if I read your note once we are on the plane? Take a picture of this moment, please.

"Yes, on the note." I humored her with my cell phone camera. "Me too," I said about this room being a special place, "I will remember it always Cathy, you make me feel like such a man, and that's not something to dismiss lightly. Now let's be off; I hate missing planes, especially one leading to a new life!"

We both laughed as I grabbed her bags and the two of us headed downstairs to the car. "I've taken care of the bill," I said, "You owe me."

"Really? Indeed I do....can I work it off?"

Smiling, I said, "Certainly, but it might take years."

"Bret, I'm figuring a session so strong that the entire amount will be eliminated in a weekend!"

"I love the thought!"

As we were loading the car, the entire Craggy Rock staff came out to hug and smile, and shed a tear or two over the "Bret and Cathy" story. It seems the account had spread throughout the entire lodge. Mick grabbed me by the neck, "You lucky guy! I'm still coming to Texas to see you, okay?"

"You bet it is okay. We'll play golf, drink some Glenmorangie, and solve the remaining problems of the world, Mick, and Cathy and I will fix you up with a Texas gal that will make you want to stay in Texas, ha!"

"I will remember that promise, Mr. Harte."

"Mick, you must knock off that 'Mr. Harte' stuff, now that you are personal friends of Cathy AND me."

"See you again soon, everyone," I called as Cathy and I got into the car heading for our new beginning in the good old U.S. of A.

At Shannon, we made it through security and into the departure lounge with no time to sit and collect our thoughts – boarding was nearly complete. Because there had been no coach seats left for Cathy, I upgraded at the gate to business class in order to sit with her. When I explained the situation to the gate agent, she said, "That's the most romantic story I've heard this month, maybe this year, so I am going to waive the normal charge to upgrade you, okay? I leaned over without saying a word and kissed the agent. "Watch him," she said to Cathy with a smile on her face.

We made ourselves comfortable in the first two seats of business class. Once we had a cocktail and the crew began readying the aircraft for take-off, I produced a piece of paper, handed it to Cathy, and said, "Darling, I think you must call her." Lori's (and Richard's) hotel was on the paper. Cathy's countenance fell.

"You're right, but this is so hard to think about."

"Just tell her you are on a plane bound for the U.S., and that you hope she and Richard can enjoy a few days vacation together in Ireland, and to call you when she arrives back in the U.S. Then hang up – you will have done the right thing with a modicum of civility and love for Lori at least, and that will be the end of her calling your cell phone for the next few days, during which time we will have our plans better thought out."

She did exactly as I suggested, and felt better once the chore was completed. "I know it sounds mean to think of screwing up Richard's entire little drama of 'fixing' things by his grandiose gesture of flying to Ireland to retrieve his marriage, but I do not care what he may be thinking or feeling. He's dead so far as I am concerned, but I do want some of his money once the divorce is settled."

"It's going to be okay, Cathy. You and I will have a life so rich and filling that the past will be nothing more than pleasant memories of the good years you did have before the ugliness."

"Oh, Bret, do you think it will be so easy?' she asked hoping for assurance.

"My dear, dear Cathy – you and I both are very strong willed people. God made the genders so different, yet so compatible in many ways. I know there will be moments of great disagreement and angst as we see some things differently, but the best, most abiding fact of our life together will be love, each for the other, great enough to overcome those bouts of anger or separation. Now you might want to read the note I left for you."

She removed the note from her purse, opened it and began to read it...

"*What a glorious morning...frustrating, but expectant with the thought of seeing you again and continuing to explore our pasts, our values, our needs, our expectations for the future, etc.*

Frustrating in the fact of awakening from my very pleasant dreams tomorrow to find that when I reach out to touch your skin, snuggle warmly against your body, and kiss all parts of you ....it is all only a dream...and now it will be hard, very hard to get back to sleep...every morning of my life until we are together.

We've begun something that I am unsure of... where it is leading...only that it all is so very agreeable...that you are so companionable, winsome, sweet, cheerful, desirable...it is scary! I have not enjoyed a day more than I did yesterday in so long a time I cannot remember. Kissing and loving you this week has awakened in me feelings I have not experienced in years...wonderful are the feelings to have a woman respond and not pull back from my advances, to kiss as good and as exciting as anything I've experienced...I am thrilled, happy, frustrated for wanting more and more of you in my arms...it's akin to the feelings of a young man who has never experienced love before and is surging inside at the prospects...

I like my life...it is settled, stable, level...no valleys...

...but with no valleys, there can never be any mountains either...and that's from where the best views come!!!

Each morning I will go back to bed wanting to find the smell of you on me....and frustrated that I can't."

Cathy began sobbing. Somewhat alarmed, I asked "Honey, what is the matter? I thought you would like the note!"

"Bret, the note expresses the most beautiful sentiments I have ever received. If I did not love you irretrievably before, I do now!"

"Well, that's a relief! I have just one question for you to seal the deal!"

"Yes, Bret, anything... what is it?"

"You're not a Democrat, are you?"

"Oh, gosh, Bret," she laughed, so loud that some heads looked over toward us. She did not answer, but simply put her head on my shoulder and fell asleep.

CHAPTER 5

The fairy tale was coming to an end when I looked out the window to a see a stormy new day in the early morning hours at Boston's Logan Airport, where we would be changing planes for the trip to DFW. "How are you this fine morning?" I asked my sleepy-eyed companion. A side note is this – even bone weary tired and without make-up, Cathy still looked prettier and sexier to me than the dolled-up women you see in the Meyerson Symphony Hall in Dallas or out for dinner in the city's restaurants, and Dallas does have some fine looking women.

"I feel like someone's beaten me with a fungo bat and I am apprehensive about the seeming monumental tasks facing me, but I am so happy to be with you on the way to Dallas. I feel like the luckiest girl in the world in one small compartment of my life at least – the rest of it can wait on me!"

"Cathy, we will get through the next few troubling months. At our age it matters not so much where we live or what we do, but that we do it together. Do you feel the same?" I asked hoping for an affirmative from Cathy.

"Bret, it's as if you somehow have crawled inside my brain and we are thinking parallel thoughts ....it's freaky how you can do that! Is it always going to be like this?"

"Yes, Honey, I think so. It's as if for the first time in my life, I have fallen hopelessly in love. What is good for you is also in my best interests and vice-versa. Certain realities will inevitably set in as we probably will have to separate for a few weeks or months getting our houses in order, but we'll make it, I promise!"

We cleared customs and traveled from AerLingus over to the American Airlines concourse and boarded for Dallas-Ft. Worth. As we waited for take-off, I said to Cathy, "When we arrive at my home, I will run you a hot tub with English bath oil and you can soak alone (or with my company), but then I want us both to have a good long night's sleep. I have blackout shades since it will still be early morning when we arrive. I am not so sure of the wisdom of showing you off to my friends just yet, in case of Richard's wanting to make some use of how easily you abandoned him. I think we need to be very careful from right now until the day you have your settlement and divorce decree in your hands."

"Bret, thank you for being so smart and attentive to details. I never received this kind of treatment from

Richard. He never thought about me or my needs, just his – those were, after all, the needs that counted. I hope Lisa gets him permanently – would serve her right. Also, for whatever it's worth – I am not into comparative anatomy or ranking sexual encounters – Lord knows I've had so very little in my life from which to judge, but you are an incredible lover. I thought sex was overrated in my marriage. It was because I had never experienced anything but Richard's inadequacy in bed, and I thought that's all there was to sex between a man and a woman. I had no idea it could be so incredible until you got me drunk in Ireland."

"Me?!! Got you drunk? If that's your story, then stick with it, because I like how it turned out." I said as I laughed all the way through the pre-flight safety announcements prior to taking off. Cathy had a keen sense of humor to go with her easy-going personality, and her patrician gait and overall sense of style. She was just perfect in every way, I thought. Why any man would risk losing her by cheating, completely confounded me, but I am glad Richard failed in his care and commitment to this wonderful woman who was still his wife until she could finalize the divorce which Richard probably did not yet see coming.

We landed at DFW on a perfectly beautiful fall morning. Traveling is not fun like it used to be with all the restrictions and security checks, but I nevertheless had enjoyed my trip home with Cathy, a situation that gave me great hope for the future. I left her at baggage claim while I went to the parking garage to retrieve my car. I had called my secretary Charlene to find out in which garage she and her boyfriend had left my car. Charlene was the best; I trusted her with many of the details of my business and personal life because she was dependable, capable, trustworthy, and as discreet as any person I have ever known. At times like this, I remembered why I pay her as much as I do.

By the time I had returned to the terminal to pick up Cathy and our bags, I saw Cathy sitting curbside looking a bit frustrated. "Darling, what's the matter?" I said, hoping nothing serious had occurred in the time I had been looking for my car.

"My bags... they did not make it out of Boston apparently. I had to file a lost luggage claim. We can go now; American will notify me when they find them."

"Cathy, it's going to be fun watching you pick out something to wear from my closet!" I said with a chuckle. We can stop at a department store and pick up whatever toiletries and personal things you need for the short term." I never stopped being amazed at how unruffled she seemed when things did not go her way.

She simply smiled and said, "Bret I am tired. Let's just go to your place – I'd love that hot bath you promised me 1500 miles ago."

I drove the 40 minutes to my home, pulled into the garage, and escorted Cathy into the house. As I pulled her into my arms and kissed her, I said "Darling, welcome to Texas and my home. You can wander about and explore while I go upstairs and run that hot bath I promised. Give me your clothes."

"Well, that's a bit direct, don't you think?"

"Honey, by the time you've finished your soak, I'll have the clothes you're wearing, washed and dried. You are certainly welcome to anything in my closet, but I'm thinking you might be more comfortable in your own things."

"Bret, you are so thoughtful. Truthfully, I do not want to think about putting anything on except maybe an old shirt of yours. More than anything I just want to soak in that hot bath and maybe have you join me, okay? There's so much to think about...I just want you to tell me you have a plan...what on earth are we going to do?....what about your job?....how are we going to be able to see one another on a regular basis? etc., etc. ..."

"Okay, my dear. There are answers to all your questions. Let's just get a bath and some rest."

CHAPTER 6

Both of us fell into my bed, each exhausted after traveling 15 plus hours. It felt so incredibly good to snuggle with this wonderful creature who seemed too good, too wonderful, too stimulating, too everything for me to believe. I hoped when I awoke that everything I had been experiencing was real and that I would not awake from a dream – how cruel that would be. I really was enjoying every moment of my time in her presence.

We both slept hard for about five hours until mid-afternoon Saturday. "Good afternoon to you, the last great love of my life," I said as I turned to kiss Cathy.

"Is it afternoon? Bret, if you are serious about your statement, then I need only one thing from you."

"Tell me and it's yours," I stated boldly.

"I need you to make love to me every day for the rest of our days together."

"Can it be twice on some days?"

"Even better! Bret, you have awakened a too long dormant libido in me. I can't get enough of your affection; your physical touch is a magical addiction that has taken control of me. Do I sound sick to you?"

"No, my Darling. You are my every dream come true. Today I cannot even imagine how incomplete my life was just a month ago before I uncovered you, no pun intended!" I guess we both have needs that the other can perfectly fill."

Cathy peered at me with the look of longing to be filled. "May I fill my daily duty now?"

"I thought you would never ask."

It never ceased to surprise me how different Cathy was from most of the women I have known. She became turned on almost instantly by my touch...even a simple kiss seemed to get her in the mood for more and more affection. Like me, she could go from 0 - 60 in almost no time. What a glorious wonder she was for me to have discovered so late in life. It seemed I was almost never able to avert my eyes from her or keep my hands off her youthful body. It felt good to be like a teenager again. We made love tenderly for what seemed a long time in the middle of the afternoon. "It is so good to be alive," I said. "Thanks, you have a way of satisfying me like no one else!"

"Bret, we are on the same page, and I love it!"

"Let's go downstairs; I'll make us something to eat, and we can begin talking about putting a plan in place for our future. I may have to run over to the store for some groceries. Anything you need?"

"You mean besides clothes?"

"Oh, right! Maybe your luggage will show up this afternoon. If not, you can put on some of my jeans, a golf shirt, and some sandals, and we will go shopping for you. But let's eat first, okay?"

I left her in bed while I went to go bathe. When I stepped out of the shower, I looked at her....she already was wearing one of my old blue dress shirts and nothing else. With nothing but her cleavage and beautiful legs showing, I suggested she was just too enticing and needed to put on something more.

"Or what?" she said as she looked intently at me.

"Honey, which one of us do you think will burn out first?"

"I hope it's not you!" she said with a mischievous laugh.

It had happened. I had found a woman who made me just want to dance every moment I was around her – like a little boy who could not get enough of his cars, trucks, fire engines, and sandbox. What a feeling!

While I was putting on some clothes to go to the store, the doorbell rang. "No one yet knows I am home...I wonder who that could be?" When I got to the door, I yelled upstairs, "Good news, your bags are here from the airline." Overjoyed at the prospect of having her things finally, Cathy came down still only in my old shirt.

"I'll get some things at the store to eat while you unpack, okay?"

With that I was off on my errand. When I returned, Cathy had gotten into some jeans, fixed her hair and face and was ready to begin preparing something to eat for the two of us.

"Soup and sandwiches sound okay with you?" she asked.

"That's exactly what I brought...an assortment of deli meats, breads, and soups. Let's eat outside on the patio," I suggested. And if you are in the mood, let's think about a timeline for us for the next six months or so."

"Oh, Bret, I so love a man who plans instead of just reacts to what life throws his way. Forgive me, but Richard was always so ill-prepared for tomorrow; he just winged it from one day to the next. You, sir, are ingratiating yourself to me more by the hour. While you were out, I read the note again you left for me with the flowers in the room at Craggy Rock Lodge when you thought you were going home alone. Bret, your note.... it's the most romantic and beautiful set of sentiments I think I have ever received. Darling, I trust you, admire you, and love you more at this moment than I could have ever even dreamed a few months ago. It's like a little girl's fairy tale and dreams come true. Please tell me I am not going to awake and find none of this to be real....please!"

"No, my dear, I think God has his imprint all over us. He allowed you to have the seat by the fireplace in Craggy Rock Lodge on the west coast of Ireland on the very night I found myself at the same spot on this planet and just a little miffed that some old American broad had already gotten the best seat reserved for herself – it was you! That has to be a God thing, don't you think?

"You must be right, Bret," she said with a smile on her face.

I brought out my most festive table cloth for the table on the patio by the pool. Cathy helped me set the table and bring out the deli meats and the gazpacho soup I had picked up at my gourmet spot. Cathy noticed, for a bachelor, I had a rather elegant collection of plates, glasses, and utensils. "If we somehow put together our two lives, we'll probably have seven TV's, four micro-waves, and table settings for a sit down dinner for 70 or 80 people," she exclaimed.

"What you described takes care of me. You mean you have a lot of 'stuff' too?"

"It's going to be a nightmare trying to downsize us both, Bret."

"Oh, I don't think so. Material possessions take on less meaning as I get older. I can live without any of it really except for a few things my grandmother left me. I bet you're the one who has the *Better Homes & Gardens* lifestyle."

"Well, I do enjoy entertaining."

"I knew it! That's all okay...I sort of enjoy having friends and associates over occasionally too. We will probably acquire an entire new set of friends wherever we set up housekeeping together."

"Where exactly do you want that to be?"

"Oh, Bret, I love the West Coast, but it will certainly depend on your work as well as what I eventually find. I would hate a long range commuting relationship."

"Why am I not surprised that we are, again, on the same page." That brings me to the next question, "Have you filed for divorce from Richard yet?"

"Yes, earlier last month. As you might surmise, Richard is contesting it. Except for Lori, I want to expunge my life with him and start an entirely new, loving, productive life. He will pay for his sins though. He wants the house, but it's going to cost him. He is in the wrong; I was faithful...a good wife for a long time. We accumulated a lot of material wealth that really does not mean much to me now. I want to be secure, have less, and enjoy the freedom of watching Lori and hopefully my grandchildren grow and enjoy their lives. Bret, you've not told me much about your family."

"Cathy, what is it you wish to know? I can give you the ten minute version or the three day one...which is it to be?"

"Let's go with the three day bio with some condensation. I'm rested and have the time if you do."

"There will probably be time for that and more in the coming weeks. What I think needs our attention most is a plan for the immediate future, say the next six months or so. Would you like to talk about a plan?"

"Bret, you are so what I need. Richard lived by the seat of his pants far too much, leaving any planning that was to be done, entirely in my lap. I would love to hear your thoughts and how we might make a go of it together."

Okay, then. Get your Day-Timer or other calendar; I'll get mine, and let's go out on the patio for our initial discussions.

"Cathy, I'm here to do anything that will help you get through the next months until the divorce is final. Do you have any idea as to the time frame for that to occur?"

"Bret, I filed almost immediately after a six months waiting period was finished. Although Richard is contesting it and making every meeting just about as difficult as possible, I have hopes everything will be finalized around April 1st." The one thing that could delay it is if Richard somehow finds out about you, and makes you a party in the proceedings. There's no basis whatsoever for it, but Richard is a conniving sort and would love to place some or all of the blame for his failed marriage on me and my supposed infidelities before he ever strayed. It's all a crock, but I'm fearful that should he ever see your face around me again after that session at Shannon Airport, he would start calculating a new strategy to save more of his wealth and give me far less than I deserve after thirty years with him. What would you say to us not chancing that?...in other words what if we put temporary time and distance between us so Richard could not possibly make any connection between us? He probably already has started checking on you for anything he might turn up."

"My darling, there is nothing you could ever do, say, or need that would cause me to fall out of love with you! I value you in my life the same as I value air and water and food for sustenance. However, I need you whole and free to love me in return, so anything you feel is necessary is okay. Being apart from you for even a day right now .... the thought is painful....but it is temporary, and when we do reconnect, it will be right and wonderful beyond our imagining."

Bret, you are so understanding. I cannot imagine us ever having a fight. I know you to be a very nurturing man, and that you would like to help me move and sort and unpack, but I'll be okay. I do not want Richard to have any opportunity to check my phone records and make any connection between us. What I'd like is to get two pre-paid cellular phones so nothing can be traced to either of us. Those phones are for private conversations between you and me; I think it will be safe that way, don't you?"

"Cathy, that's probably a good idea, I'll get us two phones this afternoon."

"Of course the first call I'll make the day the divorce decree is granted will be to you, and our life together can start. Honey, I think we might have to stay apart for six months, so the inevitable private investigator Richard hires will not be able to find anything. Can we do that?"

"My question back is, 'Do you think you will be able to handle the pent up affections I'll have in six months?' I can see us not being able to walk for three days after we meet."

"Trust me, Dear....it's you who will being crying 'Uncle' at the end of the first day and night, ha! Bret, I know it will be difficult...that's an understatement...but it will be for the best possible outcome. Are you okay with my idea?"

"When does this separation have to start?"

"Probably after tomorrow; I have to get back home to San Francisco."

"We've got no time to waste. Would you like to go skinny dipping? I'll fix a picnic lunch, and we can go on the boat to a secluded, peaceful cove I know, have lunch, rest, and swim for the rest of the day."

"Yes! Tell me more about the skinny-dipping part. If you can believe this, at my age I've never gone swimming in the buff. You, Bret, are so romantic and full of life and fun ideas. I've spent my life being a mother and a publishing professional, so I am looking forward to this next stage of my life with you! You need help with that picnic basket?"

"Sure, come in the kitchen and tell me what you like. We'll be off as soon as I ice down some drinks. White or red? Wine."

Although I love living on the water, I'd made precious little use of it lately because of my work load. Now, with a potential buyer nosing around and a relationship with Cathy on the near horizon, I could see a more peaceful, relaxed time in the days ahead with time to make use of my little ski boat which had probably no more than 40 or 50 hours on it. Cathy and I packed my English picnic blanket and basket, and locked up the house.

As we walked down to the boathouse, I said to Cathy, "I'm starting to have withdrawal pains already."

"Honey, I have something in mind that will take your focus off my leaving for San Francisco, ha!"

"That's exactly the problem! After years of being alone and having no intimacy in my life, you've unleashed a libido that I did not know was still capable of functioning, and I absolutely love you the more for it. Now, however am I to put it away for six months and go back to the cold, lonely nights alone?"

"Bret, the same is true for me. But I know that once my unpleasant past is severed legally, and I can start afresh being a full uncompromised woman, then, and only then, can we have the richest of lives together – I believe that with all my heart."

"Well, one day at a time is the course I'll have to take, but it's going to be hard...hearing your voice, but not being able to touch you, hold you, kiss you, love you, sleep beside you!"

We boarded my ski runabout, packed the picnic basket safely under the forward cowling and headed north on the lake to a secluded small island where I knew we could be alone and unobserved. It was a lovely day with smooth water. Although it was late in the season for boating, the water still maintained some warmth, unseasonably so, I thought.

"Are we really going to swim?" Cathy asked.

"I think the expression you are looking for is 'skinny dipping' and yes, we are. You'll love the water. If you get cold, I have a solution for that!" I boasted. We arrived on the beach on the west side of the island and unloaded our supplies over to a grassy shaded area where I spread my favorite blanket for our picnic.

"Bret, I can eat anytime, but a girl doesn't get a chance to go skinny dipping every day with a guy she trusts, so I'm thinking we need to go for that swim before it gets too cold or the wind starts up."

"Right you are! Hop aboard." We moved off the beach to deep water maybe a quarter mile offshore. I threw out my anchor and began to undress. Cathy seemed to be completely fascinated with the whole idea. "What are you doing?"

"The first step to skinny dipping is to get undressed," I pontificated. Cathy, who had been rather aggressive and completely uninhibited with me in Ireland, suddenly seemed a bashful schoolgirl. I simply got into the buff and jumped overboard. With some coaxing, Cathy finally took off her swimsuit and slid off the boat railing into the water – I caught her and passed her one of the inflatable floats so she could more easily keep her head above water.

"What fun," she shrieked excitedly like a youngster instead of a mature publishing executive. "What else are you going to introduce me to?"

"Lots of fun things, but nothing hurtful or too dangerous," was my response. "It will be like a prison sentence for me to be separated from you, but six months is not two or three years, it's 180 days".

"Oh Honey, let's not talk about it now, okay?" Cathy implored.

"Come here, and let me hold you, please."

"My but you are polite. It's so cold, I was coming anyway, but since you asked with a 'please', here I come," as she swam my way.

What a great feeling...was the thought going through my mind. Cathy's breasts were warm, her nipples hard, and her thighs had goose bumps up and down them. As we kissed I could see that already this quickly, Cathy was wanting me...desiring me to make love to her. Of all the things about Cathy that endeared me, I guess it was this I liked the most – she almost always was in the mood for love and warmed quickly to the physical act itself. She was unlike any woman I've known in this regard, and I loved her the more because of it!

"I'm cold. Can we get into the boat, and can you do something to warm me up?" she said with the look of a mischievous schoolgirl.

Every experience, every place, and every minute I was with her I became more and more drawn to Cathy, tied tightly to the idea of spending the rest of my life with her.

I climbed the ladder into the boat and helped her up and into the craft as well. It was broad daylight and she looked beautiful and natural in the late afternoon sunshine, just as buff as when she first entered the world. I placed several cushions and a blanket down on the floor of the boat, put Cathy on her stomach as I toweled her off. Then I lay my body on top of hers, and began kissing the back of her neck. I loved how our bodies seemed to fit together so perfectly....the next 30 minutes was the best appetizer I can ever remember. Cathy seemed to have lost her inhibitions about nudity out here on the lake in the daytime; she was intently focused on taking all of me into her and releasing tensions that had been building for years.

"Cathy, when I'm with you like this, I am no longer a man in his mid-50's, but instead a schoolboy with all the excitement and enthusiasm and hope that any man can have. Your love is so very precious to me. I am fearful of nothing in life, except anything that would separate us for more than a few days."

"Bret, I believe you are being completely honest and sincere with me. The feelings are mutual. It is pretty neat, huh?" Before I leave, we need to put a plan in place for the future...our future. Will you help me do just that?"

"Of course, my Darling. You will find me the most accommodating man in the world where you are concerned. No other woman has ever held so much power over me as you – you'd better not abuse it!"

"Here's what I'm thinking, Bret..... so there can be no charge of infidelity coming from the great philanderer, Richard, I think we have to minimize our contact until the divorce is final in late March or early April. Richard is a smart lawyer; he will be checking telephone and charge records to see who I am talking to and visiting. If we use the pre-paid cellular phones, then no one, not even Richard, can trace our conversations. If mine rings I will know it's you and no one else ever, okay?"

"That's a great idea. I can hardly stand the thought of not seeing you until the spring, but after that, no one ever will get between us...is that how you see it?"

"Absolutely, my darling." Of course, I will always have Lori in my life and will always care deeply for her as my offspring, like you no doubt feel about your son Francis. Lori will be out of school in Denver soon and on her way. I hope we all can be a great family soon. Tell me about Francis' plans."

"Well, as you know, he'll be commissioned next June in the Navy upon his graduation from the Academy in Annapolis. I plan to be there as a proud father. I would like it if you, too could be part of our June Week celebrations."

"Oh, my gosh, Bret. June is when Lori graduates from the University of Denver...May actually. Can you make it to her graduation with me? If you can, maybe all three of us can go to Annapolis in June to see Francis get his ensign bars. What do you think of that plan?"

"My darling, Cathy...you are absolutely amazing. NOTHING would please me more! I will fix it with Francis; he broke up with his long-time girlfriend last year and will likely be at loose ends. He might enjoy having another freshly minted young graduate for a companion in our June Week cabin on the Chesapeake. Is Lori attached at the moment?"

"No, Bret. She has been so dedicated a student that she has spurned men for too long. I'm getting a bit concerned. I desperately want grandkids some day. So far, she is very career oriented and has let no man get in her way. No man yet, at least, has been good enough for her."

"I like that girl already. She sounds like Francis. Maybe we can have a double wedding ceremony, ha!"

"Let's not push our luck...'one day at a time' is my mantra until I see the divorce decree."

"Okay, my darling....we have a plan...pretty simple one at the moment, but it is a start on the rest of our lives together."

I got up early and made a hearty breakfast for the two of us while Cathy was packing for her trip back to the Bay Area. During the night I had a fitful time sleeping — trying to get used to the idea of not having Cathy around for the foreseeable future. I put my feelings on paper which I planned to give her upon her departure. On the way to DFW, Cathy appeared to be feeling the same range of emotions I was – she moved close in the front seat and held on to me. I had always dreamed of a woman who fulfilled for me the whole idea of "two becoming one flesh". "My darling Cathy, I want to take a pill that will put me out for these next six months, and then wake up as we get together on April 1st."

"No, Bret, I will need you and your input during the next few weeks as Richard and I fight out the settlement details of the divorce. I know it will make me crazy – I'll need your calm, strong reassurance from time to time."

"You know I will be there anytime, anyplace for anything you need, don't you, darling?"

"Bret, I am going to get through this and be a stronger, better woman than before, especially with your help. Thank you for everything."

We arrived at the baggage check desk, and like that she was off to the concourse. Before she left, I gave her the note I had written during the night, asking her to wait until she was airborne to open it.

I drove away from the airport with a mixed emotional state – happy at the prospects for the future, but saddened that it would be several months before I could see and hold Cathy again. Today would be the beginning of laying the foundation for our future together. I would prepare my business for a sale of it; that process thankfully would likely take much of my time and focus for the time until I could again reunite with Cathy in April. If all went as I hoped, we could meet and feel totally free to pursue anything we mutually wished. I hoped Cathy would be satisfied with the idea of retiring from publishing, so we could travel and participate in cultural activities in whatever community we decide to live.

Onboard the aircraft climbing up and westbound out over Ft. Worth toward San Francisco, Cathy reached into her purse and held the note I had written for her in the early morning hours before she was awake. She smelled the note for the faintest hint of my cologne, opened it, and begin to read...

> *My dear Cathy,*
>
> *"You fear, sometimes, that I do not love you so much as you wish? My dear Girl, I love you ever and ever and without reserve. The more I have known you, the more I have loved. In every way – even my jealousies have been agonies of Love, in the hottest fit I have ever had, I would have died for you. I have vexed you too much. But for Love! Can I help it? You are always new. The last of your kisses was ever the sweetest; the last smile the brightest; the last movement the gracefullest."*
> *– John Keats, 1820 to Fanny Brawne*
>
> *In December years ago when I sat under the same tree in England where Keats wrote "Ode to a Nightingale" nearly 200 years ago, it was you in my thoughts, only I did not know your name. My*

romantic notions may never overcome your fears of jumping into a relationship with me, but a tender, hopeful place nevertheless remains inside me.

Love,

Bret

After reading the note three more times, Cathy carefully folded it and placed it back inside her purse. Her body ached from the confusing array of emotions washing over her. Deliriously happy when she thought of us and what her future might be with me in her life, but pained and fearful of the immediacy of divorce, job loss, and her short term homeless state.

CHAPTER 7

Winter had been good to me. My business had remained strong, and the negotiations for its sale had gone better than I expected. By mid-March it was done – I was no longer owner/CEO of the business I had founded back in 1988. I was not a rich man, but the $3.8 million I received enabled me to pay off the last remaining debt I had, and that was the balance I had on my home. I was finally free to move into the next phase of my life with the woman I loved. Soon she would be free to join with me in our plan for the future.

Near noon on the 4th of April my "Cathy" cell phone rang – I was a bit apprehensive; I did not want news of any delays or continuance in Cathy's divorce proceedings. She said, "My darling Bret, how soon can you be here?"

Without asking any details, I said, "Before dark today if you are to be there. I've been packed for days."

"Darling, I am free since 9:45 this morning!" she said with the enthusiasm of a young girl getting out of school for the summer.

"What took you so long? Nine forty-five was 15 minutes ago, ha!"

"Funny man! Call me with your arrival time at SFO; I have a cabin rented near Bodega Bay with no TV, phone, or neighbors nearby. Do you think we will be able to find something to amuse ourselves for three or four days?"

"Cathy, Sweetheart I have a million questions that can wait to be asked once we're settled in at Bodega Bay. The only question right now is 'What do I bring?' "

"It's cool....nothing more than a sweater, some jeans, and an appetite for food, wine, and passion. If you feel anywhere close to what I am feeling at this moment, we may kill each other...I have never wanted a man...you... as much as right now. Go get on a plane....NOW!"

Within six minutes of hanging up the phone, I was on the way to DFW. There was a flight leaving in 90 minutes that I probably could make. That meant I could be holding Cathy in my arms by 3:30 or 4:00 PST...I could hardly breathe so intense were my feelings for her and of the hot water with bath oil, massaging Cathy, and loving her until neither one of us could go on further. And a weekend of planning for the future together – that was enticing too.

The three and a half hour flight seemed like a trans-Atlantic crossing, more like 8 -10 hours than just a little over three. Finally the plane landed; I wanted to be the first one off, but it was not to be. I made my way to the terminal having telephoned ahead and told Cathy of my arrival time. And suddenly, there she was ....a vision in the same little Irish dress that I had bought for her the first day I was with her in Connemara. And she was carrying the largest bouquet of yellow roses I had ever seen outside some organized function like a wedding or funeral. This woman was alright – I indeed loved flowers, but it was usually me doing the giving. Without a word, I grabbed her up into my arms, pressing the very breath out of her in my exuberance. I just held her.... as tears welled up in my eyes.

She said, "Well that was good, but how about a kiss!"

Have you ever kissed someone for a full ninety seconds? We were beginning to cause a stir among the other travelers in the lobby as everyone slowed to stare and checkout just what was going on.

"Bret, I know you've been sitting for several hours, but can you stand another three hours driving up along the coast to the cabin I've rented for us?"

"Oh, yes Cathy ...the fresh air driving over the Golden Gate will be great. If you can carry my flowers, I'll take the bags...lead the way!"

San Francisco is such a beautiful city just about any time of the year. But on a sunny, cool spring day with just a few puffy clouds in the sky like today, it was breathtakingly and beautifully romantic. Cathy had rented a convertible for the weekend and filled the back seat with groceries, gin, and wine, and brandy – we wouldn't have to stop for a thing until Bodega Bay. Of the many times I had crossed the Golden Gate Bridge going north into Sausalito, today was the first time I had done it with the top down, looking up at the splendid towers of one of the world's best urban scenes – the Golden Gate Bridge with San Francisco in the rearview mirror. The temperature was near perfect – 68° and sunny – all with my best girl in the front seat of a little red convertible. I was thinking just how perfect everything was – I could not think of a thing I would change in my life today or this weekend.

The drive up Highway 1 was breathtaking; I hadn't made the drive in several years, but remember it as some of the most memorable coastal scenery anywhere. We did not have to stop for a thing; Cathy had thought of everything in her packing.

"Have you been here before...the place we're going?" I asked.

"No, it's a first – I have been up along the coast a few times, but have never stayed before. We'll be able to explore the coastline and the shops and restaurants together for the first time. The weather is supposed to be just as spectacular all week as it is today."

We turned off the highway onto a dirt road that ran down toward the beach protected on either side by trees. At the end was a picture perfect cabin on a point of land that jutted out into the beautiful blue Pacific – nothing else in sight, just the coastal birds, trees and some early blooming wildflowers.

As we sat in the car with the motor turned off, I looked into Cathy's eyes and said "Sweetheart, this is just what I needed...thank you. It is going to be a wonderful few days getting unwound, learning more about you, and beginning a plan for the future."

"Bret, don't think this is all so altruistic. I am in need of some tender, loving care from someone I can trust completely. These last few weeks have been hell with Richard pushing and demanding and yelling throughout the divorce proceedings. You do not turn into some kind of a demon or monster ever, do you?"

"No, never! Life is so very short. I cannot believe we have met each other and arrived at this most perfect place to begin whatever awaits us in the future. Now, what's for dinner?"

"Salmon. Why don't you open that chilled bottle of Sauvignon Blanc, and fire up the grill out on the deck, and I will have the fillets marinated soon and some fresh vegetables prepared to go along."

"Darling, I will, but first come here." I embraced her hard and held her in my arms for the longest time. "I can hear your heart beating... it's racing. Is everything alright?"

"Bret, every time you touch me I get excited and stimulated as if I was a schoolgirl being held for the first time. Promise me it will always be like this!"

Cathy, the same can be said for me. I promise it will be. We were made for each other...it just took a long time to arrive here."

"Damn you, what took you so long?"

"Cathy, all the other stuff had to come first, otherwise the magic would not have been generated – we would never have known love if our lives prior to Ireland hadn't been so bad."

We unpacked and began dinner preparations with neither of us able to keep our hands from the other – it truly was like I had just gotten out of prison after years of solitary time served with no touch or kindness having been part of my life. This time with Cathy was a tonic of the best and strongest medicine in the world, and I thanked God for every second of it.

The meal Cathy had prepared was picture perfect. With an after dinner drink nearby, I had her sitting in my lap on the deck looking out over the Pacific with waves breaking below us in an unending symphony of California coastal sounds. In the act of kissing her and touching her breasts, I felt like that teenager again experiencing all the sensual tensions of a man much younger.

"Darling, I need you. Take me to bed and make hard, physical love to me. I need you in me for hours ...for all night. Can you do that?"

And for the next six hours, that was exactly what we did!

At daybreak, I went into the kitchen and made a pot of freshly brewed French roast coffee, and took a cup with one cream, one sugar to Cathy, who was just beginning to come awake.

"My job for years was to do this same routine for Richard, and it seemed I almost never got it right. I cannot tell you how much your bringing me coffee means to me. I feel like I am a worthy person, a woman loved and deserving of being treated with respect. Thank you Bret! And, by the way, you were incredible last night; I have never experienced anything like that in my life. Where do I sign up for the continuity service contract?"

"Are you proposing to me, Cathy?"

"What if I am?"

"Well, if you are, then my answer is 'Yes!' and here's something to make it real......"

She watched me carefully and curiously as I pulled out a ring box from the pocket of my robe. Almost immediately, she began to sob....a virtual torrent...all without even looking into the box. She took it amid the tears and slowly opened it....

"Oh, Bret, you completely and constantly take my breath away. I never expected this. I hoped for it, but did not want to begin thinking it might happen for fear of jinxing my dream. Oh...oh...oh...yes, a thousand times yes!! This morning I am a princess for the first time in my entire life, and I am in love...fully, over-the-top, and forever in love with you!"

"Do you like the ring, Sweetheart?"

"Bret, it is perfect. It has the most unusual sparkle to it and it is not too big or small. Did you pick it out by yourself?

"Well, that's a relief. Yes, I did pick it out, and that's a job I do not want to have to do again – 12 different jewelers to find the stone and setting I thought would be good enough for my woman!"

"Bret, what a perfect morning! Let's go for a walk on the beach. I want to see my ring in the natural light of day."

"Cathy, have you ever made love on the beach?" I asked with a sly smile on my face.

"Someday when I do it with you will be the first time!"

"Today's the day!" And we went out for our first walk on the Pacific Ocean together.

CHAPTER 8

❧

It was a gloriously crisp, sunny morning on the ocean. As I looked at the woman I had just asked to marry me, I was astonished again at how pretty she looked after having just gotten up and dressed with not much time given to making herself pretty. Cathy had an inherent timeless clean and simple look to her that was so very appealing to me. I was used to Dallas women who were all big hair, rouge and spackle. And now I was with a woman who looked just fine with no makeup – just a hairbrush through her hair and a toothbrush for her beautiful bright white smile. It had been a long time coming...me finding someone who was a match, a soul mate, and this day I was as happy as I can ever remember. We had walked to a remote spit of land with no houses or people around. I took off my shorts and shirt, and, standing there in the nude, I asked, "Well, are you going to join me in a skinny dip or not?"

The normally prim, proper, professional Presbyterian woman, took off everything and flung them into the air

as if she was never going to need them again. I took
her hand and we plunged into the cold Pacific. Cold
Pacific...that was an understatement. Frigid was more
like the condition. Our skinny dip lasted less than a
minute. I toweled Cathy off and we both got back into
the clothes that we had cast off earlier. I led her over
to some tall beach grass behind a dune that helped to
break the wind.

"Bret, I'm freezing."

"Baby, I am going to cover you with my body and
warm you nicely, and then move you toward another
"First" on your list of things you've never done before."

"Are you sure you're not all talk concerning what I
think you are talking about?"

Luckily I had thought ahead enough to bring along
a blanket. I spread it on the grass and began to make
good on my promise. At my age, it was so very exciting
to have found a woman who enjoyed the same things I
did, and who could act with spontaneity like a teenager
again. What a morning!

As we began to get dressed again for the third time
this morning, I suggested that we needed to get back to
the cabin and begin that list of wedding time and location options.

The tide was out as we walked back toward the cabin;
you could walk for nearly a hundred yards on the wet
sand before reaching the waves. The sun was glistening

off the wet sand like a mirror with the seabirds darting back and forth – it continued to be a magical morning. A small young curious seal pup kept popping up in the bay to our left as we walked – he seemed absent of any fear and full of curiosity as to what we were up to.

When we stood inside the cabin's kitchen, I suggested that while I fixed some breakfast, Cathy should take her journal and list answers to several questions. After breakfast I would do the same in my own journal and we could begin the process of discussing all the myriad possibilities and solutions. Questions like... when for the vows, should the kids be involved, where would we pledge them to each other, i.e. church, beach, mountaintop, etc., and where would we go for a couple of weeks for a honeymoon, and where would we return to live?

"Bret, do I have to do all this thinking and listing now?"

"No, honey you do not, but when would be a better time. No distractions, no TV, no telephone calls, no chores....nothing facing us this day but doing what we desire to do. We can just get into bed for the rest of the week for all I care."

"Bret, I feel like the luckiest girl in the world! Are you always this easy to get along with?"

"Yes, I promise to always attempt to enjoy you and our life together. Life is too short to spend any of it arguing about getting our own individual way. God made the genders so very different, and I am glad that you and I are both alike and very different at the same time. I promise not to try to change you; you are an incredibly beautiful, thoughtful, strong-willed, and giving individual. I love your posture, your hands, and your ability to feel deeply about so many things. I cannot believe my good fortune to have walked ser-endipitously into the Craggy Rock Lodge in Ireland at the exact moment in time that God placed you there too and very available!"

"Very available? You make it sound like I was cheaply 'on the make'. The truth is that I was emotionally and physically drained – spent and confused. A lesser man could have taken advantage of me, I suppose...I mean I was so totally alone and lonely for the first time in my life, contemplating a new and confusing existence for myself."

"God is in charge, don't you think? It wasn't just blind luck, was it?"

"Bret, you are right, I guess. I know that I could have never invented or dreamed a scenario that would have remotely looked anything like today. We are getting married. You are going to take care of me, and I, you for the rest of our lives! What a difference a year can make. Can you believe it?"

"Breakfast will be ready in five more minutes. Will you have any entries in your journal to discuss over my omelette, bacon, and toast?"

"Alright, alright....I'll jot down some preliminary thoughts. What about you? When are you going to commit some ideas to paper?"

"Cathy, my dear, I have my list ready for you to consider. You see, I was sure that we would be doing exactly this, sure enough that I put my thoughts into my journal on the long flight out to San Francisco yesterday."

"Well, I do love a man who has a plan, and is sure of himself!"

"We eat in five minutes!"

What is better than a freshly brewed cup of Sumatra coffee after a walk on the beach in the spring of the year? I poured Cathy a cup and set her plate in front of her.

"Poached on whole wheat toast, coffee with one sugar and one spot of cream. Bret, how is it you know my tastes so perfectly?"

"Sweetheart, I observed you in Ireland...carefully, trying to get some idea of who you were. There was no sense in having to ask you how you like things when all I had to do was to observe how you ordered the first time we were together."

"You're amazing!

"Not really. But I do take notice of things that are important to me, and I determined early on that your likes and dislikes would be something that I needed to be aware of. Now about our wedding....?"

"Well, I've wrestled with the idea of telling Lori of my plans and giving her the option to bless me (us) in whatever we would decide. I love you, Bret, and do wish to have the benefit of being married to you. Although in many ways I think I owe Lori the respect of asking for her blessings, I know that right now she does not know the Francis Bret Harte that I know, and would be horrified to think that Richard and I would never reconcile and get back together. So, other than waiting for a year or two for her to get to know you, I've decided to go ahead without her permission or blessings. I'm certain that with time, she will become accustomed to the new reality of you and me and her. She can still have a relationship with Richard, and one with you as time goes by. Now what about Francis?"

"Francis thinks Ellen was wrong in what she did. He has a relationship with her, but it is not as strong as the bond he and I have developed over the years since Ellen left. Of course I have mentioned you to him, but he has no idea just how serious I am with respect to my feeling for you. I think he will be overjoyed to meet you and realize like I have, what a wonderful catch you are for someone... why not us, Francis and me? It will take him three or four whole minutes to love the idea of having you in our family. Who knows, he may even like his new step-sister, ha! So that leads us to the next question...When? And where?"

"That's two questions, my Love. As to when, I'm think-ing sometime soon after I land a job...before I start, but after I know what and where I'll be assigned. I want to live together in the same city. Would you be okay settling in with me if I got the right job in New York as well as Des Moines?"

"Cathy, wherever you are is where I am going to call home, but let's focus on somewhere warm like Dallas. What do you say to that?"

"Bret, the job market for top level publishing positions is not so fluid that I can promise I'll get lucky enough to land in Miami or Phoenix or Dallas, but anything is possible. As for the 'where' part of the equation, I have only a girlfriend, Amy and my sister, Julie, who along with Mom, I feel need to be asked to be a part of my tying the knot with you. They could come most anywhere, but it would be easiest somewhere here in the U.S. instead of some exotic locale in the south of France, and the paperwork would be easier here also. What about you?"

"Yes, I agree – somewhere stateside would be best. I have only Francis and my best friends from Navy days, Harold and Dave whom I would like to have attend. I'm thinking it might be best if we break the news to Lori.... let her be part of it, so she doesn't hold me accountable for the deed of hiding it all from her. She is the most important person in your life, right? I think it might be best for all concerned if we go to meet her soon and let her help in the planning process. Would that not work? We could exchange vows later in the summer or the fall after both Lori and Francis have graduated. Having Lori at June Week Commissioning for Francis might be something she would enjoy immensely and you too. I'll need to check with Francis to make sure that he is not involved with someone. I would not wish to have Lori feel like she was a fifth wheel."

"Bret, the more I think about it all, the more I think you are right. It would be so great for me to have a job to start in October with our move and our nuptials and honeymoon behind us. I could start fresh and with renewed energy in accomplishing something yet on the professional side of my life, especially with your support."

"So, my Dear, here we are hardly finished with breakfast on our first morning together in six months and we already have a preliminary plan on the table for our future life. Maybe the first thing we do is go to Pittsburgh and meet your mother, Evelyn. Does she know anything about you and me?"

"Oh, Bret, that is a beautiful idea. Mom is still suffering from Dad's passing, and I know she is counting on me to be a support for her. If she could but see how loving you are, I know she would be at peace with what might otherwise be viewed as a half-baked idea on my part. That's just a great idea. When would you be able to go to Pittsburgh?"

"Cathy, you know I've sold my business, and for a good amount, I might add. So I am free to go anywhere at any time."

"Well I might just want to take you home for Mom's approval when we've finished this coastal getaway. And when might that be?"

"For how long do you have the cabin rented?

"All this week."

"Well, if we could make love say 10 -15 times between now and then, I think we could be off to Pittsburgh on Monday."

"Only a dozen times in a week? Already you're trying to put me on some sort of a very limited quota for intimacy. I'm not sure I like that!"

"My darling Cathy, I do not want to wear you out or appear to be brutish. I can make love as much as you wish."

"You are the one who will wear out first. I need you! I'm insatiable right now after months of having no sex and years of not having good sex like you provide. Come here and kiss me to get my motor running so we can go upstairs and see just how much of a man you are!"

All I could do was smile as I pulled her close to me and kissed her hard with all the passion of a man who has just been released from long years in solitary confinement with no human contact. The rest of the day was given over to physical passions of two people in total love.

When we awoke in the early morning, we both were feeling the need for some fresh air. "Let's put the top down on the car and go into town for breakfast and some shopping, what do you say?"

"Shopping? Cathy, we are in desperate need for down-sizing if we are to ever fit our lives into something under 5,000 sq. ft. of living space."

"Yes, I agree that we both probably need to think about tossing 60% of our possessions, but right now I want to think about purchasing something for us together as we begin our new life. I'm thinking about a painting or watercolor of the coast. When we were driving in, I saw a gallery that might have what I'm looking for, okay?"

"Cathy, do not think I am always this easy, but 'Yes' is my answer so long as breakfast comes first."

"I love you. I think you are the world's greatest lover. You make me feel like a princess. I've never been any-one's princess before!"

And off we went cruising down California Coast Highway 1 for breakfast. We passed a 60's looking hippy place, which, of course, was the place we had to stop for breakfast. Coffee, crab omelettes, and an ocean view, all in the company of my beautiful fiancé...what could be better? After breakfast, Cathy was able to direct me to the Coastal Gallery that she had seen earlier. Inside, I found a lot of paintings that I liked, but thought they all were hugely overpriced. One watercolor in particular, named "Early Morn", impressed me. After half an hour of shopping, Cathy came to me and said, "I've made up my mind; let's see what you think."

She took me over to "Early Morn" and asked, "Well, what do you think?"

"You can't have that one!"

"And pray tell, why not?"

"It's the one I selected 30 minutes ago. Of course if you really, truly are going to marry me, then we can have it in our house, wherever that might eventually be."

"Seriously, you like it too?"

"Babe, we overlap in all the things that matter. Did you think I possibly would not love that watercolor painting of the coastal saltwater marsh at daybreak? Let me see if I can get the shop's owner to come off that ridiculous price a bit." Using my best dispassionate stance and negotiating skills, we arrived at a price that was some $500 lower than he was asking. Although it was still too much for some local unknown artist, Cathy and I became the proud owners of our first piece of art purchased together.

"It's such a nice day; I'd like to get out onto the beach again...maybe fly a kite? What would you like to do?"

"Bret, if you are going to be on the beach, then I think I'll be there too. Ready to go?"

Later as we began our hike along some rugged parts of the shoreline, I pointed to the bald eagle that was circling above. "I think we must be close to a nesting pair of those magnificent birds because he is so close and being protective. Maybe we should do our kite flying further up along the beach."

I had purchased a box kite earlier in the day during our shopping. We stopped at a likely spot with some strong wind to assemble the kite. "With these winds, the kite might just lift you off the ground," I said to Cathy with a mischievous smile.

"I agree. You had better be the one to hold the string, and I'll launch it." We had 500 feet of some fairly strong nylon kite string and were able to get it all played out quickly. What a day of pure relaxing it became as we walked along the beach with our kite sailing high above the trees and shore.

An hour into our adventure, Cathy asked, "How would you like to go to dinner down the coast a ways and feast on some of the best oysters and fish you've ever had?"

"Would it be you that I would have for a dinner date at this feast you're proposing?" I responded.

"Yes, Bret, I think that's the general idea. Are you game?"

Well, then...yes, I'd like that. You wear your ring, and we will celebrate our first dinner together as an engaged couple. And where is this destination...what is it called?"

"It's Sam's Cove Fish & Oyster Bar, and you will love it."

Reeling in the long line of kite string, we began to start the trek back to where we had left the car.

Back at the cabin, I drew a hot tub for Cathy with some English bath oil. As she eased into the very hot bath, I asked, "Save me a spot opposite you, okay? I'll bring you a glass of wine and a sweet smelling candle."

Cathy smiled and said, "Don't be long...you haven't held me all day, not since this morning anyway." I eased into the hot tub behind her, and began to massage her neck and shoulders. "I'll give just two hours to stop that," she said with a laugh in her voice.

"I loved this woman, and could hardly observe any sense of decorum by keeping my hands off her in public. I simply devoured her using my hands to do what I could not achieve with my mouth. No spot on her body went untouched by me, yet very softly throughout. I could tell she was enjoying my touch, and ready for me to take her, dry her off, and put her into bed underneath me. I wondered if it would always be like this with her – I could not get my fill of her.

We showered, dressed, and took a leisurely drive southward along the coast. It was late afternoon and the views were stunning as we looked out over the beautiful Pacific with the waves crashing on the beaches.

"Cathy, I think we need to decide if we are going to go to Denver to tell Lori of our plans. Maybe it would be good to celebrate your birthday there with the three of us over dinner. We all could plan our coming back for her graduation in May and see if she would be interested in joining us in Annapolis for Commissioning Week Ceremonies for Francis."

"Bret, Darling, that sounds like a good plan to me, but there's one thing you need to be aware of...Richard will be at Lori's graduation directing everything for his little angel's commencement. It will be difficult to say the least. He will not be happy to see me, especially with you."

"Cathy, it sounds like we have our work cut out for us....I mean between now and then in getting Lori comfortable with what she will need to see as inevitable – that her mother and I, Bret, will be a pair into the future and forever after."

"Oh, Bret, it is going to be hell. I don't want to think about it tonight. I know you are right, and that things will work themselves out eventually, but it will be a storm once Lori hears about us."

"Okay, Sweetheart. We'll not talk more about it tonight; we'll just have a good dinner and drink some wine, and enjoy the gorgeous weather and each other's company. How much farther is this Sam's Cove place?"

"We're nearly there. It's an old northern California saloon on the water. There's a large painted nude above the bar, and surly old waiters in white aprons who, for the most part, have been waiting tables there for 30 or more years. It's become a bit touristy over the last few years, but we should be alright tonight – most of the tourists will not be arriving for another few weeks."

Suddenly, there it was – Sam's Cove Bar and Seafood House. It looked like a stage set...an old rundown, but stable bar and dining room jutting out over the bay with water views on three sides.

"This is going to be fun," I suggested. "What are you in the mood for, Babe?"

"What I'm in the mood for is not on the menu, Bret!" Cathy shot back with that mischievous smile that I was becoming addicted to.

"Well, I think you'll have to settle for something that is on the menu. I'm thinking of some oysters, and something that I can't get in Texas, like abalone."

"Yes, that's good. You eat a couple dozen oysters in the half shell, because you're going to need it later tonight and tomorrow!"

"You weren't kidding about being ravenous, were you?"

"Bret, you have turned on a monster. I've never had feelings like I've been having constantly since meeting you. I hope you are not becoming bored or tired or overwhelmed by these feelings, are you?"

"Honey, you are every man's dream...a beautiful, slim, active, hot natured, intelligent woman who appears to be in love. If someone offered me a chance to change anything about you, I couldn't find a single thing, except maybe that I would have met you before Richard."

"No, I think you are wrong. Meeting you first without the long, frustrating years with Richard probably would not have prepared me to be so totally energized and committed as I now am. The timing is God's – it's just perfect for both of us...that's my thought anyway."

"Okay, maybe you are right. Let's eat."

"Maybe I'm right? Maybe you're going to pay for your own dinner tonight!"

We were given a table waterside, the perfect spot to watch the sunset as we ate. And Cathy was right. The food, atmosphere, and drinks were just the best. Here we were, seemingly miles from anywhere, having a romantic dinner as a couple that did not exist just a little over six months ago. I'm afraid I went a bit too far decorum-wise, touching Cathy at every opportunity, and kissing her often while at the table. I asked our waiter, "We're not embarrassing you, are we?"

"Oh, no, Mr. Harte. You are good for our business. Everyone wants to have a romantic rendezvous. I think half the restaurant is envious; you are a beautiful couple, who seem very much in love. Is this a special anniversary or something?"

"Well, Tom, I met this woman on vacation in Ireland six months ago, and we have just now re-united. She even agreed to marry me yesterday, so we are on an emotional high that might never end, Tom."

"Mr. Harte, if I had a lady as pretty as you do, I think I would be feeling the same way. Congratulations!"

We finished our crème brulee and coffee, and paid the bill. Taking our glasses of port out to the wooden pier, we walked to the end. The moon was full, the evening cool, but still and quiet. "Promise me it will forever be like this, Bret!"

"Sweetheart, I think this white hot heat we're constantly feeling will either consume us or burn itself out over time. But what I think will be left is a loving comfortable happiness that will be even better. What do you think?"

"You're probably, right, Bret, but this schoolgirl excitement about the future being with you....well, I do not want to lose those feelings. I never want to fall back into a life of quiet frustrations and unachieved dreams."

"Cathy, you likely will be a grandmother before too long. That circumstance will open still another horizon for you...for us. Life is going to continue to get better and to educate us further, I promise."

"My darling man....I love you so very, very much. Let's drive back to the cabin to see if those oysters have given you renewed stamina, what do you say?"

"If we were on horses, instead of the car, I'd say, 'Let's race back!' "

Back at the cabin, we made love for hours with the passion not even teenagers could muster. So far, I liked this 'being engaged' routine.

CHAPTER 9

❦

The plan for the next few days was laid out. I felt the need to meet Cathy's mother, Evelyn Schuyler to pay her the respect of asking for permission to marry Cathy. And the big unknown was Lori, who was still waiting for Cathy to reconcile with Richard. Cathy called Lori in Denver to make plans to celebrate her birthday there at the family's favorite steakhouse with Lori. As soon as the reservation number of three came up, Lori wanted to know who else was coming. Cathy explained that she had someone she wanted Lori to meet. Lori was very apprehensive, but after an hour's conversation long distance, she finally acquiesced to a celebratory dinner on the weekend before Cathy's actual birthday on Wednesday.

"Bret, I am so looking forward to getting together with Mom – she's going to like you as much as I do."

"Is she as pretty as you?" I asked.

"Prettier and smarter without the benefit of a master's degree," Cathy said with a laugh in her voice. "Now Mom will be irritated if we stay in lodgings other than her house. Of course, since we are not married, it will be expected that you stay in the guest room, and I likely will take my old room upstairs that I had when I was home from college in my Penn State days."

What we had decided was to go first to Pittsburgh for a couple of days to visit with Mrs. Schuyler, and then to fly back west to Denver to smooth the way with Lori. "Do you think Lori has any idea of what is going on?" I remember how pretty she was during the brief encounter we had at the Shannon Airport – an all-American-girl-next-door look coupled with a youthful exuberance.

"She has been alerted that I am seeing someone, but does not know that it is you. She's just disappointed that her wishes for her parents to get back to life the way she remembers it – because that's not happening, it has her upset; she's a first born, actually an only child, and I guess to some extent I, and Richard for sure, spoiled her. She is going to need to find out about life – that it is not always so idyllic; that serious hurts happen in everyone's life, even hers."

Monday our flight to Pittsburgh from San Francisco was on-time and uneventful. Cathy and I traveled well together, I remember thinking. She watched for and retrieved our bags while I was picking up the rental automobile. We loaded the vehicle and were on our way in record time.

Although I was driving, Cathy knew the way and directed me patiently as I missed several turn-offs on the expressway. When we arrived, you would think it was two sisters meeting instead of a mother and a daughter – such was Mrs. Schulyer's youthful appearance. She immediately came over to me, took my hand, and said "Cathy has an excited schoolgirl smile in her voice whenever she mentions your name, so I guess it's serious between you two." Looking back over her shoulder towards Cathy, she said, "My, but he's a polished and fit looking gentleman, Cathy. Welcome to my home, Mr. Harte."

I liked her...a lot. Her smile and warm handshake made me feel welcomed, and enabled me to feel relaxed immediately. I could see Cathy in twenty years when I looked at Mrs. Schulyer, and I liked what I saw. "Please call me Bret, Mrs. Schulyer – it would help me relax."

"Alright, Bret. I hope you like roast. We'll be having dinner an hour and a half from now. Would you like to freshen up before that? And can you make a good, dry martini, Bret?"

"Yes to both questions, Mrs. Schulyer, that is, if you have some Beefeater gin and fresh vermouth."

"I like him already, Cathy" was Mrs. Schulyer's immediate response. "Well, Cathy can show you to your room and the bathroom you'll be using. When you are ready, Bret, come back down to the parlor, and make us a pitcher of your best martinis – I've not had one in

months. The bar supplies are in the hutch over there,"
as she pointed across the room.

As Cathy walked me upstairs I grabbed her shoulder
and said, "Well, so far, it sounds like I'm on solid ground
with your Mom."

"Yes, I'm a bit surprised how she seems to have taken
to you right off. That's not her usual style around strange
men interacting with the family. It's a good omen for
when we decide to unveil our plans for us."

The house was a century old Victorian manor with
a wide wrap-around front porch, complete with a
hanging swing, baskets of colorful flowers, humming-
bird feeders, and a stunning view of the valley to the
west. I was impressed with the beauty of the home site
and the level of caring attention it obviously received on
a regular basis. I reminded myself to comment on those
things to Mrs. Schuyler over cocktails.

After unpacking and attending to details of hygiene,
I slowly went downstairs to attend to my bartending
duties. The cabinet was fully stocked with a variety of
liquor and cordial types that would be the envy of any
uptown bar. By the time I had my pitcher of martinis
mixed, both Cathy and her Mom entered the room,
ready to begin the evening's happy hour at home.
Everything seemed so very comfortable to me, almost
like I had been there many times before and was just
returning home like Cathy. Mrs. Schuyler suggested
we go out onto the porch since the weather was so very

pleasant. I took all three drinks and some snacks I had found on a tray to the outside.

"Mrs. Schuyler, you have such a beautiful and comfortable home. How are you managing it all so well, now that you do not have your Jim?" I asked trying to compliment her. Of course it prompted her to tear up and begin a short reminiscence about what a good man her late husband was. Jim too had been a naval line officer when they met during the Korean War when he was home on leave.

"Jim was such a perfectionist about his yard and flowers and home upkeep. I will not ever let it get rundown – that would make Jim sad if he should see it happening from his view on high."

"Mrs. Schuyler, ..."

"Bret, I very much appreciate your southern manners, but please call me Evelyn. It makes me feel younger when a young man speaks to me like I am a contemporary of his."

"Thank you, Evelyn. I'm sure the condition of your home and garden would cause Jim to smile – it looks really beautiful. I am interested in the photograph on the wall of Jim's study. Can you tell me about it?"

"Oh, that's Jim in uniform in front of the Officers' Club in Pearl Harbor – he had just made Captain and was being given command of the USS Iowa. As you

might imagine, he was pretty excited to be back on the
Iowa, having served on it fresh out of Annapolis in 1940
as a newly commissioned Ensign. He was a real good
commanding officer. Cathy told me you too are an
Annapolis man, is that right?"

"Evelyn, I would so much have enjoyed meeting Jim
and talking about his experiences in World War II and
the Korean Campaign when he was commanding the
battleship. What an experience! Yes, I graduated in the
class of 1980 and got out of the Navy as a Lt.Commander
to go into business. There are days I wish I had stayed
in, but the continuous sea deployments took a toll on
my marriage. However my son, Francis, is graduating
this June, Class of 2010. I am so proud of him – he's the
Brigade Commander and headed for Nuclear Power
School and the submarine service this fall."

As our little initial "meet & greet" happy hour continued, I felt I was getting to know a lot about Cathy from
the experiences Evelyn was relating from years before.
I could tell she was enjoying herself and the evening
immensely. It apparently had been quite awhile since
she had any meaningful reminiscences to enjoy with
people who cared. With dusk approaching, we made
our way to the dining room to begin an almost formal
dinner with the best full lace Royal Copenhagen china
on the table, candles, fresh flowers, and beautiful silver
and crystal serving accompaniments. Clearly, it seemed
to me that Evelyn had a goal of impressing me or honoring me by all the work that had to have gone into this
very special dinner.

The meal of pork roast and all the trimmings was just superb. A special bottle of champagne Evelyn had been saving for her and Jim's next New Year's celebration was served which helped further the flow of conversation over a wide range of topics. Clearly Mrs. Schuyler was well -travelled and equally well-read, and conservative in her politics. I was liking everything about this woman, and especially her adult daughter, Cathy. By the time we had finished and were about to go into the parlor for a glass of port and coffee, I was feeling relaxed and as full of joy as I ever remember feeling in the past.

"Evelyn," I asked, "do you take in tenants? I mean how much would you charge me to live here? Everything is so perfect!"

"Well, Bret, if you develop a strong enough relation-ship with my daughter, you would not have to pay a thing for any time you wished to stay with me. "What do you say to that?"

I, probably looking overwhelmed and searching for words, said "Evelyn, your beauty and graceful spirit make me very, very happy. One of the things I had hoped was that our meeting might go well, that you could see me as a man totally in love with Cathy and everything that is a part of her life. My goal was to work up enough courage to ask for your blessings to marry Cathy and care for her and all of you forever. You have made that action very easy for me. I want to blend our two families together. May I have your consent to begin a life with Cathy by marrying her?"

There was complete silence. Her laughing and smiling, happy demeanor were no longer visible. I held my breath. What if I was mis-reading the evening so far? It would be no way to start our marriage if Mrs. Schuyler was not onboard with the idea.

After a full two minutes of uninterrupted silence, Evelyn rose from her seat, came over to me, reached her arms around me, and said, "Yes, I would like that.....a son that Richard never was nor wished to be."

Relieved, I hugged her and almost picked her off the floor with my glee.

"Have you set a date, Bret?"

"No, Evelyn, we still have the big hurdle of bringing Lori into our decision. She is not even aware of me or this thing we are proposing – marriage to her Mom. Our next move is to go to Denver on Friday and see if we can convince Lori that Cathy Harte will still love her and be around for her as we go forward."

"Bret, that will take some selling skills and lots of patience, but I am convinced it will eventually work fine. Please do not give up easily. Lori is a smart young lady and will eventually understand why her Mother loves you as she does, right Cathy?" she said with an impish grin. "Lori loved Jim and, as his only grandchild, he spoiled her with attention. He wanted her to go to Annapolis, and she almost decided to apply, but some teenage romance spoiled those plans, and she went to Denver instead where Richard, her father had attended.

Bret, you have Annapolis as your ace in the hole. Lori will be impressed with that."

"Thanks for telling me that about Jim and Lori. I will put it to good use as we go forward. Take care of your-self. If everything works out the way we hope, Cathy and I will be back here to celebrate Thanksgiving with you. Would that be okay?"

"Oh, yes Bret, that would be great. I will have some-thing to look forward to all summer and fall. Happy Birthday, my darling daughter. I will be thinking of the joy I was experiencing some 50 years ago next week as I was giving birth to you."

And so ended my first visit to Cathy's childhood home – as I hoped, only better. I felt I had a new Mother in my life as well as a new friend. Now we were off to our largest challenge yet –Denver to reveal our plans to Lori.

CHAPTER 10

I t was beautifully clear, but a little colder than I had expected when we landed in Denver. We rented a car and drove directly to our hotel to get ready for meeting Lori and a friend for dinner. During the flight Cathy and I had discussed Lori's state of mind with respect to the divorce and the revelation that Cathy was seeing someone. At this point, Lori knew nothing nor cared much about who the new man might be in Cathy's life.

As we were unpacking, Cathy suggested that on the telephone Lori has sounded distant and divorced from the reality that Cathy was unmarried and no longer a part of the nuclear family that Lori had always known. "Perhaps it would be better for me to meet with Lori tonight alone and attempt to smooth the way. She still has some lingering frustration and anger over my leaving her in Ireland with Richard last Fall after they both had traveled so far to see me. Richard and I spoiled her; she has always gotten whatever she wanted

by asking or appearing to be hurt if we went against her
wishes. Unfortunately, that history has not given her the
skills to navigate the real world. But she is older and a
smart individual, who, I am hoping will use her reason-
ing abilities to see my view of the future as it impacts
her. Would you understand if I did that tonight, Bret
– see Lori alone?"

"Sweetheart, you need to know two things..... first, it
pains me to be away from you in a beautiful new place
for us even for just a few hours, and two, that I value
your judgment enough to always allow for my needs to
fall into second place. But just don't make it a habit,
okay?"

"Oh, Bret, how ever did I find a man like you? I do
deserve some goodness, but you transcend everything
I've dreamed and hoped! Thank you. I am going to
meet her at her condo, and from there we will go out
for a quiet dinner someplace where we can talk for the
first time alone since before Ireland. Some fences need
to be mended, largely by me since I have been out of
touch with her for a lot of the time during the divorce
proceedings."

"Go. Do you want the car?"

"No, but you can drive me, and if I am late, I can take
a cab back to the hotel. You will have the bed warm,
won't you?"

I took her to Lori's place near the university, and
returned to the hotel room. After ordering room

service, I took out my journal, and began the long task of updating it – it had been months since I last put any thoughts into it.

I must have dozed off at some point in the evening. Someone knocking at the door wakened me. I looked at my watch; it said 1:15 AM. When I opened the door, there was Cathy, all red-eyed and exhausted looking. "I'm sorry Darling, but I forgot to take my door key. You're still dressed; could you not sleep?"

"Well, come in here and let me hold you while you tell me about your dinner with Lori."

"Oh, Bret, it was not at all what I had hoped for. Lori is still up to her tricks. She invited Richard to Denver to celebrate my birthday once she knew I was coming. Poor child! She still wants with all her heart for me and Richard to reconcile our differences and get back together."

"Richard was at dinner?" I asked incredulously.

"Please don't be mad, Bret. He was, and it was tense. Although he was trying to be on his best behavior, cracking jokes and trying to be friendly....touching me on the arm and stuff, I just wanted to get back here to you. But we did go to dinner. By the end of the meal, Richard, who is an alcoholic, was feeling on top of the world, Lori was happy, and I had relaxed some. I did explain to Richard while Lori was in the bathroom, that I had fallen irretrievably in love with someone else, and would be getting married at some point this year.

Richard was drunk, but sober just enough to realize that his plans were dashed finally. He asked if you were here in Denver. I did not lie to him – 'Yes, he is here,' I said. Before I left in a taxi, he asked if he could meet you."

"Cathy, Sweetheart, I am so sorry. Tell me what you are thinking about my meeting Richard and that is what we will do."

"I was with him for nearly 30 years. I just want it all to fade into the past, and allow me to go forward with the new life you and I have in front of us."

"It's your birthday weekend celebration. We will do exactly what you would like, but because you spent 30 years with the guy, I am curious about him. Although I am backing you completely, I would not mind meeting the guy."

"Okay then. I will call Lori and tell her we'll meet her and Richard at the steakhouse tomorrow night – actually tonight, right...it's already Saturday? But Bret, I want my birthday celebration to be memorable and romantic, just the two of us, so you'll need to pick some place for us to have dinner Sunday night to celebrate alone."

"Consider it done. You call Lori, and I promise to find you a great meal with wine and dancing in Denver to take your mind completely off the past. Now I have a birthday present for you. Would you like to receive it after our dinner together Sunday night or now so you can wear it in front of Richard?"

"Oh Bret, I still cannot believe how lucky I am to have met you. You are extraordinary! Richard makes a lot of money, and I would rarely get a present, sometimes not even a card, on my birthday or anniversary. The answer to your question is "Yes, I want it now! I do not want to appear petty, but wearing anything some man other than him has given me would be just grand theater."

I produced a small beautifully gift-wrapped box and gave it to Cathy. She immediately became transformed into an excited little girl as she opened the gift. Once opened, she shrieked and jumped onto me like some puppy, just happy to see me, and kissing me all over.

"Bret, I love it. The very idea of jewelry on my birthday is enough to get you some sexual favors tonight (this morning), but this diamond necklace is over the top. Come, let's go to bed. I want to undress you and have you undress me, and then have sex all night until the sun comes up!"

"Whoa! Don't you realize that you have chosen to be with a 55-year-old man?"

"I'm sure you are up to a special performance this morning, and I can't wait. Let's go!"

Although it was her birthday, I think I got the better gift. Cathy had become as wild, wanton, and uninhibited as any man could dream. Our morning in Denver was the stuff of legends. Gosh, I loved this woman!

In the late afternoon as we were getting ready for the big dinner and meeting with Lori and her dad, Cathy said to me, "Bret, I'm nervous about seeing Richard again. He'll be charming until he's had a few drinks. I really want a pleasant evening for Lori as she meets you. I think it's best if we remain calm throughout allowing for our happiness and joy to become evident. Richard will likely become brash with his idea that something of his was taken from him, and that you are responsible for vandalizing his family and his life. If it does get to that, I hope neither of us responds to those ludicrous ideas he'll probably be spouting as he drinks more and more as the evening wears on. Darling, I want Lori to see how wonderful, how calm, and how genuinely caring you are, and that alcohol plays no debilitating role in your life. Can you do that for me?"

"Sweetheart, it's your birthday. I'm looking forward to meeting Lori and drawing her out in conversation. Let's plan on the time being a good investment that will ultimately pay dividends if we're patient."

"Okay Bret. You're ahead of me again – I so love that about you."

We arrived exactly on time to the steakhouse, a somewhat elegant but rustic-looking place in the hills west of town. Coming inside, I noticed the hostess was expecting us or Cathy, at least, and escorted us directly to where Lori and her father were seated. Richard appeared different than I had remembered – he actually was a tall, well-groomed, handsome man, over six feet tall wearing a beautiful silk jacket over a dark turtleneck sweater underneath. He and Cathy made a good looking couple back a few years ago was my initial thought. He reached out to Cathy to kiss her hello as she turned her head so Richard was left only to kiss her cheek. "Poor guy" I remember thinking – he has come to realize the enormity of his loss. Cathy immediately introduced me to Lori as Francis Harte and then to Richard the same way.

Richard said, "I thought you went by Bret."

"My friends and associates call me Francis; I am called 'Bret' by my immediate family since I was a little boy growing up in East Texas."

Lori pressed in, "Mr. Harte, I remember you from Ireland last fall. You were with my mom at Shannon Airport. Would you care to bring me up to date as to what is going on?"

"Why, yes Lori. We have a casual dinner ahead with time to talk about anything. Are you excited about becoming a freshly minted college graduate soon? My only child, Francis, Jr. is just three weeks behind you, graduating from the Naval Academy in Annapolis the first week in June."

Lori let down her defensive tone just a bit. "You have a son graduating from Annapolis? I almost went there!"

"Yes, I know. Your grandmother told me of Jim's wish that you would have followed in his footsteps as his only grandchild. Your mother could not go because women were not admitted to the Academy until the class of 1980."

"You've seen my grandmother?"

"Yes, and she's very proud of you."

Richard was feeling left out of the conversation, and interjected, "Francis, when did you see Evelyn?"

"Richard....may I call you Richard? We just left Blue Sky yesterday. Evelyn mentioned you several times." I did not say it was for his being an alcoholic jerk that his name came up in conversation. Cathy almost laughed out loud – she knew exactly to what I was referring.

"Lori," I said, "why didn't you go to Annapolis? I think you would have cut quite a figure in a naval officer's uniform."

Lori was softening. "Thank you Mr. Harte. You're right, but Daddy went here to the University of Denver, and I had a boyfriend (who turned out to be a jerk) that also was going to Denver for his Hotel and Restaurant degree, so here I am four years later with a business degree."

"Have you ever been to Annapolis to visit?" I asked Lori.

"Oh, yes, I did get to go once with Granddad. It's a lovely historic 18th century town on the Chesapeake. You've probably been there a few times visiting your son Francis...is that his name?"

"Lori, I've been there more than that...I'm actually a member of the Class of 1980, and consequently, am very excited about Commissioning Week for Francis. But what excites me most is coming back to Denver in a month to see you walk across the stage to receive your degree and some graduation honors, right?"

Richard chimed in, "Well, I guess we'll just have a big party again in four weeks."

Cathy could not help herself..."Richard, will you be bringing Lisa or is she not divorced from Roger yet?"

"Oh, Mother, stop it!"

Richard interjected, "Lisa has run off I'm told to the big island of Hawaii and is living at 50 years of age with some young blonde surfer bum. So no, I do not think any of us will be seeing Lisa anytime soon."

"Richard, you could fly out there and probably reha-bilitate her." Cathy was obviously enjoying making Richard pay yet some more for his indiscretion last summer before I met her.

"Mother! Stop it please." Lori pleaded. "Can't we just have an adult, pleasant dinner conversation?"

I squeezed Cathy's hand underneath the table to let her know I thought she was going a little outside the bounds in her needling Richard. About the same time Richard knocked his drink over into his lap, and had to excuse himself to go to the bathroom to attempt to blot up the damage to the expensive silk sport coat he was wearing, now wet with his cocktail.

I whispered in Cathy's ear, "I know he deserves it, but can you ease up just a bit? I do not want Lori to be unhappy at the end of our first evening together." Cathy nodded compliance.

"Lori, what are your plans immediately after gradation? I mean, I would love to fill you up with the world's best crab cakes in Annapolis in early June. I'll give you the best tour of historic old Annapolis that you will ever have. And you will love the cottage I have rented right on the bay in Edgewater Estates — within kayaking distance to the Academy and downtown restaurants across the bay, if the water is still."

"You better check that invitation with your son," Lori said skeptically.

"I will if you are interested. Francis and I are very close – more like brothers than a Father /son relationship – we think alike. We... your Mother, you and I... can talk more about it when we are all assembled back here for your graduation next month. I think it would be even more fun with you there with us."

"Mr. Harte, I do not yet have a job going into the summer; consequently money is tight. I'm not sure I could swing such a trip right now."

"Lori, I'd appreciate it if you'd just call me Bret. There's no financial considerations for you to concern yourself with – I'm taking care of all the expenses for Francis' Commissioning Week party. It WILL be a grand party, made all the more special by your presence! Will you promise to think about it, please?"

"Has Francis even met my mother, Bret?"

"Not yet, but I know my son; he is going to enjoy her – what's not to like about Cathy?"

"You got me on that one, Bret. She is a pretty special person. And with that I'd like to propose a toast to C. S. Lewis." We all raised our glasses. "To the best example of a mother a child could have on her birthday, may we all be grateful."

"Hear, hear!" I said. This evening was going better than I had anticipated. Richard was not the drunken, angry boor I had expected, Cathy seemed to be relaxing somewhat, and Lori was enjoying herself as the center of attention. Ordering dinner, I said to the waiter, "I and the lady on my left will have the lamb with loganberry glaze, asparagus, and mashed potatoes."

"How long have you been eating lamb, Cathy? I've never seen you enjoy it before," Richard asked.

"Richard, there are a lot of things you never discovered about me in the nearly 30 years we were together. Bret's knowledge of the world has helped me discover things about myself that even I did not know."

Dinner went longer than either Cathy or I had anticipated as both Richard and I talked about our careers
and personal histories. He, Richard, was not so bad a
guy as I had fabricated him to be in my mind for his
selfish, ego-centric ways. He seemed to be a changed
man since losing the most precious thing in his life, his
wife, lover, and friend, Cathy. I was actually beginning
to feel sorry for him.

With dinner being over and the hour getting late, we
assembled in the restaurant foyer to say our good-byes.
Richard took my hand, shook it, and asked me to take
care of Cathy better than he had. And Lori, perhaps a bit
high from all the cocktails and wine, hugged my neck,
and said, "Were you really serious about me coming to
Annapolis in June?"

"Yes, I'm very serious. When we next meet, I may
already have the airline tickets for you and Cathy both,"
I said with a smile on my face as I hugged her back. Now
you ace your final exams, okay?

As we were driving back to the hotel, I asked, "Well?
What do you think, Sweetheart?"

"Oh, Bret, it went so much better than I had hoped.
I believe Lori actually likes you too. And thank you for
drawing her out in the conversations; she loved being
the center of attention, despite it being my birthday."

"Yes, now about your birthday. Where do you want to
have dinner to celebrate – just the two of us?"

"Home at my apartment in San Francisco. I want you to cook your Steak Diane recipe again for me, and make love to me in front of the fireplace – that would be the best celebration I'm thinking."

"Done! Let's fly back tomorrow after brunch on whatever flight is available. We are certainly making a dent in our frequent flier mileage programs, aren't we?"

During our flight back to San Francisco on Sunday afternoon, I gently broached the topic of Richard. "Cathy, will you please tell me what you are thinking about Richard after our dinner last night...I mean everything went pretty well, don't you think?"

"Yes, it went better than I ever could have imagined."

"Do you hate Richard?" I asked with a tinge of regret in my voice.

"No, but I hate what he did, and I'll never trust him as I did for all those years we were married. I thought I was the luckiest girl in the world for a large part of my life with him, despite his addiction to alcohol and to his work."

"The reason I asked is that he seems to have realized what he has lost, and I guess I'm feeling a little sorry for him. If I should ever lose you, I would go mad, and not ever be able to endure a social evening with anyone, let alone the man who was taking you away from me."

"Bret, what is going on? You know that you would never cheat on me, and certainly not with my best friend. I have forgiven him, but it's very difficult to forget what he did. His infidelity did allow me to find you; I guess that's a plus in the whole scenario."

"Cathy, I guess I am easing toward asking you something that will cause you to question my stability."

"Whatever are you talking about, Bret? You're not sounding like yourself."

"Cathy, I have talked to Ellen twice in the last six months. Time has healed my angry state with regards to her. What I'm thinking is that she and Richard might be a match. Would that be something that you could tolerate?... I mean if I somehow put them in touch with each other."

"Bret, I think you are actually serious," Cathy said with a look of incredulity.

"Well, Sweetheart, I am, if you're okay with the idea."

"Bret, what dividends would your meddling in their lives possibly pay?"

Maybe you're right; maybe I should just drop the idea. Ellen was always enamored with attorneys since her father and grandfather were in the legal trade or profession. I do not dislike her, and would like to see her happy with someone, but she doesn't ever venture out or do the online dating thing. She may die just as she is now unless someone helps her find her 'Mr. Right'... that's all I'm thinking."

"Bret, why am I not surprised? Did you bring home every injured bird and mouse you found and nourish them back to health when you were a boy?"

"You figured that out, huh?"

"Well, Bret, I won't stand in your way, but please do not get me involved with Richard, okay?" You are too good. I hope someone helps you as much when I die and you are single again."

"Now cut that out!"

We landed at SFO amidst some fog which was actually in the process of burning itself off. A friend of Cathy's, Jenny Linehan, had promised to pick us up at the airport so she could meet me and hear the details of all that was going on. We drove to Cathy's new apartment; I had seen nothing of Cathy's life or living arrangements in San Francisco, and was quite interested in where and how she was living now since the divorce. We crossed the Golden Gate Bridge, an experience that always leaves me breathless – it has to be one of the best urban views available anywhere. We continued up past Sausalito and turned east toward Tiburon. Driving along a rather secluded lane, we turned into a condominium development of Cape Cod style homes. Cathy's address was #30 Mendocino Lane on the corner of San Simeon with a view of the Bay. For a flat lander like me, the home, the site, and the neighborhood was impressive. Jenny was the first of Cathy's friends that I had met; I liked her – she would ask questions and actually listen patiently for the answers and not chatter on and on as I presumed women would do after a long absence from one another. She also had the good intuition to know that Cathy and I had a lot to do after returning from our trips up the coast, to Pittsburgh, and to Denver; she excused herself after depositing us at Cathy's door. I commented to Cathy on what a thoughtful friend Jenny seemed.

Inside I took Cathy in my arms and just held her. We already had been through so much in so short a time, and there still had not been that first argument or stressed feelings at all. "I love you, Sweetheart more than I ever thought I would be able to love again. You are so beautiful in body and in your soul – I am so very, very, very fortunate to have found you at long last. Thank you for a wonderful few days. Now do I have to stay in the guest room?"

"Oh, Bret, the guest room would be such a far commute for me several times a night, I think we might both be served by your staying in the master suite with me so I can take care of your every need, and a few of my own at the same time."

"Well, I'm glad that sensitive issue is settled."

"Bret, I hope you'll begin to think of this as your home, our home on the West Coast. It's not too feminine in decor for you, is it?"

"Cathy, I am still looking for something, anything that I do not like about you and your tastes. It amazes me how alike we are. Your tastes are better defined than mine from a decorating standpoint, but I love every wallpaper, drape and countertop in your home. There's even one countertop I like well enough to lay you down on it and have my way with you."

"My darling man, there's not a room or closet, love-seat, or chair in this house that will miss a loving act with you....that is my hope for the future. I am going to take a hot shower and unpack. If you would like, check your mail on my computer in the office, and then come up to the bedroom. I'll have my hands warmed and some hot fragrant lavender oil ready for a massage of your tired body that you will not soon forget."

"Cathy, that sounds perfect. Isn't it too early to go to bed?"

"It's my birthday tomorrow, and getting into bed with you now is what I want. Humor me, please," she said with a wink as she headed up for her shower.

The woman knew how to please me and keep me interested. I almost felt like I was losing my manhood and independence, so in love and captivated was I by this woman. While she was in the shower and unpacking, I looked around, exploring the house or home that I likely would come to know well in the coming weeks and months ahead in my relationship with Cathy. I found the all important utility room with its washer and dryer – that's what I needed after two weeks on the road. While I was doing my laundry, Cathy had emerged from the shower, put on a pair of jeans with one of my old shirts she had confiscated, and gone to her neighbor a few doors down the street in order to retrieve her mail for the days she had been away. Suddenly I heard shouting, happy whoops coming from Cathy's office. I came out to see what was causing the commotion.

"There you are! Are you alright? Have you found your way around my place?" Before I could answer, Cathy was holding up an envelope and a letter that she apparently just opened. "Bret, you are going to like this news almost more than I. You had better sit down!"

"Well, okay...it is good news, right?"

"Oh, Bret, it's fabulous news or can possibly become fabulous with just a bit of negotiation on my part."

"Yes, yes....what is it, Honey"

"Bret, remember me telling you about the dozens of resumes I had sent out during the time since I got back from Ireland?" Without stopping for my answer, she continued, "Most all of them were to publishers back East in New York, a couple went to Des Moines, Iowa for possible opportunities within various *Better Homes & Gardens* publications, and one went to a new start-up publication in Dallas. Well, of all the responses, only one came back with any real interest in me and what I had to offer for the immediate future. *BH&G* has something coming in about a year that they would like to talk to me about, but the one immediate opening is in Dallas with a new magazine called *Senior Living and Travel.* This letter is an invitation to come to Dallas for an interview with the principles concerning my becoming their editor-in-chief. You're not involved in getting me on the short list are you?"

"Oh, Cathy, that's almost too good to be true! And no, I know nothing about this new publication."

"Well, they want me to call at my earliest convenience and set a meeting date for a first interview in Dallas. I may just accompany you back to Dallas and look seriously at the prospect of living in Texas....oh God, I cannot believe I just said that!"

"Does that mean that you're throwing me out, making me go home to Dallas?"

"Well, let's see what we might be able to work out. I'd prefer not to stay in a hotel if you would be so kind as to loan me a bedroom at your place."

"Cathy, the master bedroom is yours anytime for as long as you need it. My neighbors are sure going to wonder what is going on, though. There hasn't been a woman coming or going from my house in several years."

"It's my birthday. I think the first thing we do is go to dinner to discuss all these potential developments, and then have a nightcap and some dancing at the Top of the Mark. What do you say to that?"

"Let's do it. Do you mind calling for the reservations while I finish getting my laundry folded and organized? Where are we going? What'll I need to wear?"

"Chinese, and you will need a coat and tie?"

"For Chinese...I need a coat and tie?"

"Sweetheart, the Chinese restaurant is in the middle of Chinatown. It's my favorite – better food and safer food than you can get by traveling to China. The coat and tie is for later when you take me dancing at the Top of the Mark in the Mark Hopkins Intercontinental Hotel. Have you been there?"

"Not with you, Darling. I'm going to enjoy this evening as much as you."

"It's a bet, but I don't want to hear about any other woman you've taken there, okay?"

"Not to worry. It was my early days as a young naval officer when I went there for a nightcap and looking for any unattached ladies. I found a table of white haired little old matrons who danced my feet off until the place closed."

"I do not believe a word of that story, Bret, but it sounds good enough to let you off the hook for tonight."

Out of respect for Cathy and her special day, I put on my best new sport coat, gray slacks, and a bright tie. When I looked in the mirror, I had to admit that I was still a pretty good looking guy. Cathy noticed and said, "Are you the guy who's going to accompany me on my birthday celebration tonight?"

"Yes, I am. And Ms. Lewis, may I say you look ravishing...beautifully delectable! I am going to have a tough time keeping my hands off you!"

"Who said anything about you keeping your hands off? We must display some small sense of decorum, because I want to be able to go back to my Chinese place...I mean you cannot, under any circumstances, have sex with me in their dining room, understand?"

"Aw shucks, Lady....you're asking a lot of me tonight!" I liked Cathy's sense of humor; she would always carry her playfulness with me past the normal boundaries, and cause me to laugh. "I have to warn you, you arouse me just about any time with your clean, healthy All-American, 'girl-next-door' look, but tonight, in that dress that I've never seen, you look awesome. We may not make it home from the Top of the Mark. Have you ever stayed there?"

"No, it's way too expensive!"

"Well, so is fighting a morals charge for having sex on the dance floor. We may wake up in the morning in a suite at the Mark Hopkins."

"I think you're all talk! Come on, I want to order you a dinner that you will long remember! I bet there are some things you've never eaten before!"

"Remind me to tell you about Escape and Evasion School in Panama back in my military days. I killed and ate raw just about anything that moved in the jungle down there, but you may be right about the Chinese." As we were heading out the door for Cathy's car, I said, "Just to be safe, why don't you grab a toothbrush, some makeup, and a fresh blouse and pants." She looked a little confused. I have my shaving kit and a clean shirt, so I really do not have to bring you home, if you work your birthday magic on me like you do most any other time." Cathy smiled, kissed me, and said, "I'll not be but a minute, you bad man!" as she raced upstairs to get her overnight bag.

We had a wonderful evening. Cathy was right about the Chinese restaurant; the owner knew her and served us up a never ending buffet of some of the best food I've ever eaten. Cathy was exuberant – happy because it was her birthday, a potential job offer was on the horizon, and she was in love. At the end of dinner, she was ready to go dancing. She had called ahead to her favorite place for nightcaps – the Top of the Mark – where we had a table waiting against the windows with a stunning view of the nighttime skyline. Although we had not been separated for two weeks, I was able to have a birthday gift hidden in my jacket. In Denver I had given her a small diamond pendant necklace which she wore to dinner with Lori and Richard. Its presence on her there had caused some conversation and excitement as a birthday gift from me. It scored points with Lori because they both liked the design of it a lot, and the idea of a present from me was a red flag waved in Richard's face. Tonight after we ordered our first round of nightcaps, I produced another small box and gave it to Cathy.

"What's this?" she asked excitedly.

"Is today not your birthday? Do you not usually receive something for your birthday from the person that loves you the most?" I asked her with a smile on my face.

"Bret, I am happier at this moment than I can ever remember being in my whole life. You gave me a beautiful necklace in Denver. That was enough – too much actually – a diamond necklace! Whatever am I going to do with you?"

"Well, for starters, you could open that," I said pointing to the gift box. When she opened it, she started crying.

"Bret, the necklace was just stunning – I love it so much, and now these earrings to match....you are too generous. However am I going to repay you for your thoughtfulness?"

"How about a slow dance or two every night for the rest of my life starting tonight?" I suggested. The trio on stage was playing an old Mel Torme song called "That's All". We danced and danced until finally I wanted this woman as much as I have ever wanted anyone. I asked the club manager to get us a room in the hotel, and he graciously took care of everything. I paid the bill while he was arranging for a key to be brought up. I took Cathy to the room, and while she was getting ready for bed, I went to the car in the garage for our overnight bags. When I returned, Cathy was waiting for me in the bathrobe that was provided in the room. She was more than primed for an evening of lovemaking not to be forgotten. I think I got the better of the gift giving on this particular April 21st.

The next morning we sleep late and ordered breakfast served in our room. There was much to be discussed concerning the upcoming calendar for the next month and a half. Her job interview needed to be scheduled in Dallas, plans made for our attendance to Denver for Lori's graduation, and later in June for Francis' Commissioning Week activities in Annapolis. It looked very much as though we would be living out of suitcases for the next six weeks. We made plans and synchronized our digital Day Timers; there was much to be done, but I calmed her with my resolve to help her get it all accomplished on a timely basis.

"There are two questions yet to be resolved. First, how would you feel about living in Texas?" I asked with a real interest in knowing her answer, and second, "When do you want to be married? I was thinking around the first part of September, so we could honeymoon in Ireland on the first anniversary of our meeting in the dining room at Craggy Rock Lodge."

"Oh, Bret, the simple answer is 'Yes' to both possibilities – it almost sounds too good to be true on the one hand. The publisher of *Senior Living and Travel* needs what I have to offer, but we haven't talked about compensation yet. I will not settle for a pittance just because it's Texas and not New York."

"One step at a time, my Darling. Get him to like you and your abilities and your contacts, and the money you need will come is my guess. And remember, you already have a place to live....he probably does not need to know that however. I think you could hit the ground running with me in the background to support you."

"And love me?"

"That goes without saying!" I exclaimed.

"I still want to hear it – all the time. Remember Richard was too busy to bother. And before I forget, thanks for a wonderful birthday."

We had covered a lot of terrain last night and today – now to make it all happen.

CHAPTER 11

❧

W e spent two entire days at Cathy's house packing for all the eventualities the following month and a half might present. She would have to pack for job interviews in Dallas plus graduation ceremonies and parties in Denver and Annapolis.

In one month we had to be in Denver for Lori's graduation and two weeks later in Annapolis for the same event for Francis. I asked Cathy to set preliminary planning for Lori's function while I would do the same for Francis' Commissioning Week. Then we would put the schedules together to make final airline/hotel/car rental reservations for both of us for both trips. All this traveling had to be worked around Cathy's interview with her prospective Dallas employer.

Richard was planning a big post graduation party for Lori and her friends and any parents who were interested in attending – a garden party at one of Denver's country clubs. Of course Cathy and I were invited guests.

For the extended weekend revolving around Francis'
graduation, I had already a year ago rented a waterfront cottage in Edgewater, MD across the bay from
the Academy. Cathy and I would be staying there and
hosting a similar party after the commissioning ceremonies – a really grand clambake that was to be catered
for any and all of Francis' friends and a few of my old
classmates who also had sons or daughters in the class
of 2010.

My present to Lori had to be discussed with Cathy,
and she then would have to alert Lori to the intended
gift. I wanted to give her an all expense paid trip to
Annapolis to attend the June Week festivities with us
and stay in the cottage with us all. I had thought Lori
might object or have other plans for the weekend just
two weeks after her own graduation. It turned out that
she did have tentative travel plans, but she actually liked
the idea of seeing Annapolis as an insider with me, her
mother, and was interested in seeing Francis get his
Ensign bars. Frankly I was surprised, but very happy that
Cathy had sold Lori completely on the idea. Neither
Lori nor Francis had met one another, but both were
curious since it was becoming increasingly apparent
that her mother and I were quite serious about pursu-
ing a future together. I thought the kids would erect
some sort of barrier or make some fuss about bringing
an outsider into a family event, but I was very pleasantly
surprised that both Lori and Francis thought it was a
good plan. I sent each of them photos of the other.
Cathy told me the response she received back from Lori
was positive, and Francis too thought Lori looked 'suit-
able' – whatever that meant.

I love it when a plan comes together as easily as this one seemed to be happening. Cathy was also surprised, but thought it was testimony that God's hand was all over our intended marriage.

We had no more than just arrived in Dallas on Monday afternoon when Cathy received a call from the publisher. He apologized for his delay in setting an initial interview date, but asked could she make it on this upcoming Friday morning. She informed him the timing was good since she had just landed in Dallas for a visit with 'friends', and that Friday morning would be fine.

Cathy was an experienced professional; I was surprised how calmly she was taking the interview prospect, especially with all that was riding on it. The job was right here in Dallas. A successful interview and job offer would solve a huge amount of problems with respect to her landing quickly on her feet and being almost instantly productive – no searching for a house, no real packing or move to worry about initially, and few expenses when viewed against a move to New York City for her and me.

We both began an intensive few days of research on the company and its principals and investors to make sure the job was a right fit for Cathy and her rather impressive resume. By Friday we had enough information on hand to believe that the job would be worthwhile for Cathy. It was not difficult for Cathy to look the part of a big city editor or publisher for that matter. She looked very businesslike in her blue suit as I drove her downtown to an impressive office tower address where the interview would be conducted. I kissed her good luck and suggested she could call me when she was finished – I'd be at The Adolphus Hotel waiting in the restaurant for her.

It was three and one half hours later that she called. "Can you join me for a drink?" I asked.

"Sure!" She sounded happy. Since we were both dressed in suits and it was near the dinner hour, I had made dinner reservations right there in The Adolphus Hotel in "The French Room", one of Dallas's toniest rooms for special dinner occasions. When I pulled up to the building and saw Cathy, I pretty well knew that she had aced the interview.

"When do you start?" I asked with a big smile on my face.

"Buy me a drink, and I will tell you everything."

"Sure thing!" I said as I pulled up to the hotel. "Do you feel like a celebratory dinner downtown, Sweetheart?"

"A little later, yes. First I want to unwind, tell you about the job, and ask your impressions."

We walked up to the bar which is a perfect place to discuss business...quiet, just a piano softly playing up front and with a real 'clubby' feel with wood paneling and large historic portraits on the wall. "Do you feel like champagne?" I asked.

"Sure, Bret...let's celebrate, but nothing expensive... no Cristal yet, ha!"

Once the bottle I ordered had been presented and we had our flutes ready, I proposed the toast, "To you, C.S. Lewis, to your success, and to your lasting happiness in whatever you undertake."

"Thank you, Bret. That is special. Have I told you lately that I love you?...a lot?"

"No, but it's always good for a guy to hear from so lovely a woman as the one I'm sitting with."

"Let me assure you, sir, that you can likely get lucky tonight, even without diner in The French Room."

"Well, Cathy, let me hear all about what has you in so good a mood."

"Bret, the interview was a piece of cake; it was thoroughly enjoyable – I liked the principals and the head guy to whom I'll be reporting if I accept the job. They definitely need somebody like me if they are going to make it. It's a startup with no one really possessing even a rudimentary knowledge of what publishing a magazine and making it profitable is all about. They sensed that I had the experience, personality, and drive they were hoping to find, and actually offered me the job, subject to one more interview with the entire team of investors who they feel need to be totally on board with the selection."

"I hope you did not give them your answer yet, did you?"

"No, Bret, of course not for two reasons. First, the money they are proposing for the position is way too little for the work and the skills they are needing. Second, I am not easy to impress nor as available as they might think. Of course, on the personal level concerning you and me, it would be just about perfect – headquartered right here in Dallas with lots of traveling likely required, most of it to Central and South America as well as to various U.S. advertisers' headquarters. You and I could see a lot of places we could investigate for retirement, all for the readers of *Senior Living and Travel.*"

"Cathy, our life together is forming up beautifully. I thought it would be harder than this."

"Bret, if I make this move, and ever catch you cheating on me, I'll kill you in the most painful way any Muslim ever thought up....do you understand me, Dear?"

"Oh yeah, right! With the cravings you have, the demands you place on me, I'd be too tired to ever be able to get it up with another woman."

"Are you complaining? I thought you liked our chemistry, the physical part of us."

"I do, I do, I do! Cathy, I never want to ever say 'No' to you. What I have is every man's dream. You look, smell, act, speak, and carry yourself with that special grace that seduces me every time I see you. I'm in love totally and forever for the first time and the last time in my life. Now that's way too much confession of my most inner feelings. The one of us who loves the least, controls the relationship – that's the part I'm still trying to figure out."

"Oh, Bret, you are wonderful! When do you think we will have our first fight? I cannot believe we are such clones of one another mentally. Physically, there is one difference between us that I like a lot."

"Now cut it out...you are getting me aroused and it's way too early for that."

Cathy laughed. She knew exactly how she could get my motor running and straining almost anytime, anyplace. Actually, that certain seductiveness was one of the things I loved about her. "Before we go in to dinner, I want to know if we can honeymoon in Ireland on the first anniversary of our meeting at your table in front of the fireplace in Craggy Rock Lodge?"

"Bret, just book it, and we will back up all our plans to that time. Now feed me so I can still be awake and nourished enough for the passion tonight that we both need, okay?"

Cathy had never been to downtown Dallas and certainly not to The French Room. When we walked into the dining room, I heard an audible gasp from Cathy. She had traveled all over the world, seen a lot of places, eaten in some top venues, but The French Room with its vaulted, frescoed ceiling still impresses, and it did its job on her even before we sat down.

"Bret, this is lovely. You could not have picked a more appropriate venue for tonight's dinner....I mean I am on the verge of becoming a TEXAN of all things...that's meaningful, right? I never, never thought when I was growing up in Pennsylvania that someday I would fall in love with a Texan and live way down there, much less be calling myself a Texas woman! Funny how things work out; life just continues to educate you, doesn't it?"

We had an exquisite dinner. As a finishing touch for her successful interview, I ordered Crepes Suzette prepared table side for the two of us. It had been a long day. "Before we call it a night and head for home, can I have a dance or two?" I asked.

"Bret, you are ever the romantic, aren't you? Of course, I'd like to have two or even three dances with you."

Things were coming together nicely, I thought as we were driving back to my home in the North Dallas suburbs. "Tomorrow, Darling, we should talk about plans for Lori's graduation and the gift or gifts we should give her."

"Tomorrow will be fine for that, Bret. Tonight I just want to lean on your shoulder and sleep a little until we get to your house."

During the weekend we made our reservations for Denver for Lori's graduation weekend, and bought the presents we were to give Lori for achieving her degree. Cathy's idea was a matched set of leather luggage and a European trip. I opted for a leather briefcase and covering the costs of her trip to Annapolis, if we could convince her to join us at the June Week cottage I had rented. In less than a month we would find ourselves back in Denver to see Lori graduate and probably have dinner with her and her father Richard. Cathy was not looking forward to that part of the weekend; I was okay with it – Richard did not seem the ogre to me that he did to Cathy, but I did not have the nearly thirty years experience and wasted investment in the marriage that she had.

CHAPTER 12

No sooner had we landed in Denver and checked into our hotel than Cathy's telephone rang. It was Lori checking to see where we were in our travels. She was excited to find Cathy already in town. "Daddy is here too and wanting to take us all to dinner," I heard on the speaker phone.

"Well, Sweetie, I am here with Bret, and we can join you. What time and where are the reservations?" Cathy asked.

"The Steakhouse, our old hangout, of course and 7:00 o'clock," was Lori's excited response.

"We'll be there, Lori," and hung up the phone. "Oh, Bret, I so wish we could do this celebration without Richard's presence!"

"Darling, it'll be fine. It's about Lori and her graduation, not about us or you and Richard. I know being around him when you want to forget all the hurt is difficult, but I'll try to keep him busy talking about his legal conquests and empire building, so he'll not have much time to bother you, okay?"

"Bret, you are a dear!"

We arrived a little early at the restaurant to get a drink into Cathy beforehand so as to settle her nerves. Our timing was good. Just as we were finishing our cocktails, Richard came in with Lori and one of Lori's friends. Seeing us in the lounge, Richard came over, greeted me cordially, and tried to kiss Cathy. Cathy turned her cheek letting Richard know that he was now a virtual stranger and not her lover anymore. I could not help feeling sorry for the guy – 30 years invested and now all of it was gone. True he brought it upon himself with his infidelity, but I, as a man, could not help but feel his pain. I should feel indebted to him actually, because if he had not strayed, my future would have looked so vastly and woefully different. Regardless, Richard was in a generous, happy mood – his only child, a beautiful woman was graduating tomorrow with honors from a difficult economics program at the university. So tonight all restraint was thrown to the wind – Richard was treating for steak and lobster and all the extra courses anyone wanted.

Richard was in charge and began ordering with a flourish, starting with two expensive bottles of wine, one Sauvignon Blanc and one Pinot Noir. He was restrained enough to begin asking questions of Lori about her favorite memories from her days at Denver, favorite courses, professors, etc. and moved into questions about her hopes and dreams for the future. Lori seemed to be loving every minute of the attention, spoke long and well about her experiences and feelings.

The evening progressed smoothly through the vichyssoise, pate de foie gras, table side preparation of Caesar salad, and the beautiful porterhouse steaks and huge lobsters for each of us.

After finishing Lori's favorite dessert, Bananas Foster, for us all, Richard presented Lori one of her presents – a full day of spa treatments at one of Denver's ritziest salons.

The evening was finished. It all had been lovely and over-the-top expense-wise. After saying our good-byes to everyone, we attempted to leave, but Richard asked me to have a nightcap in the bar with him – Cathy and Lori could have a few minutes for girl talk and visiting. I accepted, probably against Cathy's wishes, but she went along with the idea. I ordered my usual scotch and soda, Richard some port, as we began a conversation about the future, something he obviously was curious about. I could not dislike the guy. He was smart, very articulate...could have a career in politics was my thought process concerning him. He asked if Cathy was okay. I, not wanting to provide any information without Cathy's acquiescence, said, "Richard, she was hurt, but is getting over it all. We plan to marry this fall sometime."

"Bret, I've done a lot of foolish things in my life, but none so painful and just plain stupid as being unfaithful to Cathy. I regret it terribly, but am glad she has found you. She seems happy, and I'm confident that you will care for her as much as I did, and not fail her... ever."

"Richard, that's kind of you. Have you found someone for yourself?"

"No Bret, I haven't. I have just immersed myself in my work hoping that more time and attention in that area will bring some measure of success and peace."

"Richard, may I ask you something of a very personal nature?"

"I suppose so. What is it?"

"In my design business, I have been a very good net-worker over the years between my clients and friends. The reach of any individual is very much greater if he but makes as many friends and contacts as is possible. What all this is about, I can sum up with this question for you. I actually like you enough to introduce you to someone who might be a match for you. Like you, she is classy, articulate, well-traveled, divorced for a number of years with one adult male child, and Richard, she is much prettier than you!"

Richard laughed. "Bret, I hadn't really thought much about dating, but it's probably time. How do we go about this introduction?"

"Good, Richard. I really think the two of you might hit it off. Let me talk to her, and when I'm through building you up to her, she'll say an enthusiastic 'Yes!' I'm sure."

"Bret, why this interest in my well-being?" I'm a little surprised.

"Richard, I guess I too am surprised that I find myself liking you instead of despising you. If we had met any other way, I would like to have built a friendship with you and maybe have a reliable golfing partner for some club tournaments. I probably should go and break up the girls' conversation. Tomorrow we can talk further about setting something up with Ellen."

"Ellen? I like that name."

"Goodnight, Richard. And thanks for allowing me to be part of your dinner this evening. I've got this bar tab, so you can go retrieve Lori."

Driving back to the hotel, I asked Cathy how Lori was feeling about her big day tomorrow and the evening's activities we just completed.

"Bret, she is happier than I've seen since Richard and I split. I think she even likes you because of how happy I am with you. And best of all, you and Richard seem okay with one another, so Lori is comfortable with everything. I asked her about coming to Annapolis for June Week and she seems to be in the mood for it."

"Good! Cathy, I, too, probed Richard a bit to see how he might feel about being introduced to Ellen. Of course, he doesn't know who Ellen is at this point. He said he would look forward to meeting her if I vouched for her. Of course, I built her up to Richard, but the bottom line is I think they might hit it off. Ellen is a little stuck up and always wanted to be married to an attorney since she came from a line of them. So, at some point, I will find a way to introduce them to each other."

"Bret, Darling, I like that you are a 'happy ever after' kind of guy, but this whole plan makes me squeamish. You do whatever it is that you're driven to do, but please keep me out of it. Richard has been such a louse during the divorce. I can't see myself ever being comfortable around him again. Okay?"

The rest of Lori's graduation weekend went smoothly; the weather was clear, warm, and sunny. Lori, of course, was the center of attention and she was loving every minute of it. Richard gave her a graduation present of a cruise aboard the Queen Mary 2 to Southampton and a three week rail pass to explore Europe and then a flight home to San Francisco where she could camp out until law school began. Cathy had prepared Lori for our gifts of luggage and a trip to Annapolis in two weeks for another graduation celebration...this time for Francis. Lori was happy about everything and excited about the upcoming summer.

Before we left Denver, I asked for some time alone with Lori to tell her about my plans for us all in Annapolis. I told her I planned to ask Richard to come also and her job was to sell him on the idea. Lori was puzzled by my plan to ask Richard to Annapolis. "What has possessed you Bret? Asking my father to be with us in Annapolis? I do not understand to say the least."

"Lori, I'm playing matchmaker. I have a friend who will be there and I'm betting your Dad would like her...a lot. If you will trust me on this, I am going to plan on it happening. Richard has said he would be amenable to meeting someone of my recommendation, he just does not know when or where. Will you sell him on the idea of coming to Annapolis? I promise you a good time and having your father there will be good for you and him, and I think he will like the woman I'm going to introduce to him. Your father needs a good woman in his life instead of fretting about Cathy for years. I plan to take good care of Cathy, and I am hoping you will acquiesce to your father dating again after his divorce. Lori, I know this all sounds a bit cracked, but it could turn out to be a load of fun. And I'm also hoping that you and Francis may enjoy one another's company. Francis is a lot like me, and you are a lot like Cathy. Who knows how much fun we all might have in Annapolis? None of the graduation party is composed of anyone who's genuinely unpleasant to be around – it'll be a long weekend of crab cookouts, historic tours, sailing on Chesapeake Bay, and just us all getting to know one another better. You certainly need to know Francis – at the very least, he'll become your step-brother this fall when Cathy and I marry. What do you say? Will you sell Richard on coming out to Francis' Commissioning Week?"

"Well, Bret, Mother has said that you are a fun guy to be around. You do seem high energy and full of fun. I'm going to trust you a lot on this scheme you've cooked up. I will get Daddy on board, but I want to hear more about this woman you're going to introduce to my father."

"Tell you what, Lori. When Cathy and I get back to Dallas, I'll call you and tell you all about her and the weekend's accommodations. It's going to be a grand time – almost as good as your graduation was this weekend. I'm glad it has all gone so well for you. 'Bye, call you tomorrow!"

On the flight home to Dallas, Cathy said she had spoken to Lori about coming to Annapolis and surprisingly enough, she was somewhat in favor of the idea, excited actually. I told her that I had also spoken to Lori earlier today and enlisted her help.

"Whatever for? I mean what can you possible need Lori to do?"

"Now hear me out, Cathy. It's pretty crazy, I'll be the first one to admit, but I've asked Lori to sell Richard on the idea of coming too."

"WHAT? Have you taken leave of your senses?"

"Sweetheart, you said my introducing Ellen to Richard was okay, did you not? Ellen is going to be in Annapolis for Francis and for his commissioning. Rather than have her nosing around me and you constantly, I thought Richard might be just the right distraction for her and for you as well as me. Neither Richard nor Ellen have been around another potential partner so far as I know for some time, Ellen for a long time. Ellen is pretty, smart, articulate, and has always wanted to be married to an attorney. I'm counting on Richard's testosterone to kick in and charm the socks off Ellen. Who knows, maybe they'll hit it off. We can both hope, right?"

"Bret, you are toying with fire and with other people's lives. It could blow up in our face, then what?"

"Darling, what if it doesn't? Have you ever heard of a more unique set of interpersonal relationships? Boy meets girl. Boy's father likes girl's mother; girl's father likes boy's mother, and they all lived happily ever after! Have you ever heard a fairy tale better than this one?"

"Oh, Bret, I think I'd better have Dr. Whitson give you a thorough checkup – you've lost it!"

"Maybe so, but you've got to admit, it's going to be an interesting weekend in Annapolis!"

CHAPTER 13

With just over two weeks left before we needed to be in Annapolis for Francis' Commissioning Week activities, every minute of time was taken in planning for the momentous changes that were in the offing – Cathy's new job negotiations, planning her relocation and transition to Texas, shopping for June Week, and coming to terms with Richard being in such close proximity for a week, and thinking about the future after the excitement of graduation is gone for Lori and Francis.

I took charge of all arrangements for travel and accommodations to Annapolis. I made Cathy promise to trust me as I figured out the best plan for all of us. After talking to Richard and explaining my ideas to him, we came to an agreement on what might work best. I booked Richard into the same B&B in Eastport across the river where I knew Ellen had decided to stay. She loved the old historic B&B, having stayed there several times over the last few years. I was lucky to know Amy, the proprietor, well enough to get Richard placed in one of her best rooms, probably the last good room in all the area for Commissioning Week, when thousands of proud parents and relatives come to watch their son or daughter throw their head covers into the air signifying the end of a four year grind. I also spoke to Lori and suggested she stay in one of the cottage bedrooms with us so she and Cathy could be together. The cottage was not really a cottage, but instead a rather large single house retreat right on the bay.

Ellen, my ex wife, knew that I had found someone, that fact revealed in a letter I had written her after returning from Ireland. I, too, had communicated in a subsequent letter that I had sold my business and was planning to marry the following year. Although Ellen did not love me nor wish to be in my life in any way other than to be one of Francis' parents, the news of my probable marriage surprised her after so long a time of us both being single. I asked her if she would be bringing anyone along to the June Week festivities, and that I wanted her to meet Cathy as well as Lori. She stated that she was coming alone, and that she would like to see who had captured my heart. My plan was that we all would get together on Wednesday evening after arriving in Annapolis for a leisurely evening of cocktails, my famous clam chowder, and crab cakes in the backyard of our June Week cottage – she could meet Cathy and Lori, and Francis would be there to do the same thing. I did not tell her about Richard, but had a pretty good feeling that the two of them, Richard and Ellen, would probably find enough common threads and chemistry to make the weekend work just fine. Finally, I suggested shorts and Hawaiian shirts would be the uniform of the day for the evening's activities to begin our June Week celebrating Francis and his big day on Saturday.

After I got everyone's acquiescence to the Annapolis plan, Cathy suddenly began to take a strong interest in making everything 'over-the-top' perfect. "Could we go into Annapolis a day early for me to get the lay of the town, the cottage, and to get everything set up for the weekend?" Cathy asked expectantly. "Sure," I said, "that sounds like a great idea." I had anticipated problems, and was surprised that everything seemed to be coming together without mishap.

Cathy was scheduled for her final interview with the investors of *Senior Living & Travel* on Friday before we were to leave for Annapolis. Because the job was so important a part of our future... a senior editor/publisher position of a magazine headquartered right here in Dallas, we spent many hours discussing the particulars and researching the market for such an endeavor. It seemed to me that there was indeed a strong market for seniors and their leisure needs. The situation was a good fit for Cathy's abilities and our need to be in the same town once we married. One of the surprising aspects for me was just who were the individual investors and board members of the new magazine. I knew by name several of the principals, and one happened to be a good friend, retired Army Brigadier General Royce Reardon, with whom I had worked on Veterans Affairs legislation a few years ago – he was a good man and conservative proponent of taking care of our wounded and mentally damaged soldiers, seamen, airmen, and women who had served our country. I liked Royce. He would likely be surprised to see me in the company of his new magazine editor and publisher, all a big plus in Cathy's favor.

On the day of the final interview, Cathy was dressed in her best suit, confidently ready to go downtown and meet the men who would be ruling on her employment. She was surprisingly calm and confident. I commented on her totally professional look and demeanor. "You do not seem nervous at all, Sweetheart – just supremely confident and ready for a new challenge."

"Bret, I am. Thanks for saying so. These guys need someone exactly like me if they are going to make *Senior Living & Travel* successful early on."

"Honey, there is no one exactly like you, so I guess you're hired, ha!"

"Bret, I am not going to work as hard as I know I will have to, put in the hours, and make them all a lot of money without the package we've discussed. I want a piece of the magazine. If they balk in the least, I may just say, 'No, thanks, Gentlemen!' " The compensation I am asking may sound like a lot to these Texas boys, but it is more than reasonable by New York publishing industry standards. If they hire a younger, less experienced individual, it will cost them their investment in this terrible economy."

"Good for you, Cathy! Go get 'em."

I drove her downtown to the location that had been selected for setting up the offices. It was a good, if not inexpensive location with a top floor corner office designated for the new Senior Editor/Publisher. I escorted Cathy up to the 17th floor and wished her good luck. I would wait for her in the outer reception area until she came out of the conference room.

It was 11:00 o'clock when she went in to the interview. I began to get antsy when she had not come out at 12:30 p.m. The receptionist, a young, but polished and sharp woman in her late twenties, offered to show me where I might get some lunch. Just as I was listening to her suggestions, Cathy came out, and asked me to join her in the conference room.

When I entered, the first face I saw was that of General Reardon. He immediately came over and gave me an almost affectionate handshake and hug. "Bret, this lady has cut herself a very lucrative deal, and all the board is confident that we have found our Editor-in-Chief for *Senior Living & Travel*. She was intimidatingly good at negotiating her performance contract. I trust we shall be off and running sooner rather than later with her at the helm."

Cathy took my arm and introduced me to all the board at one time, "Gentlemen, this is Francis Bret Harte, the Dallas businessman whom I met in Ireland last Fall, the same man who has asked me to marry him this Fall in September. When we set the location, gentlemen, you all are invited."

General Reardon said, "Bret, can you join us and our new editor for lunch at the City Club?"

"Yes, General, and the champagne is on me!"

As we left for the short drive to the Club, I kissed
Cathy, and said, "Sweetheart, you do everything with
such grace and style. I am so very lucky to have you in
my life. Congratulations! The board seems wowed by
you....just like me!"

"Bret, I cannot believe how my life has turned since
meeting you. Just eight months ago, I was drained,
despondent, and fearful of even my own shadow. I had
not been alone and unemployed ever before in my
adult life. I was angry and lonely. Even Richard and his
cloying apologies were beginning to sound reasonable
and maybe the proper approach for me. THEN I went
to Ireland to think and read and cry and explore, and
the second night I saw you sitting alone in the dining
room at Craggy Rock Lodge. I thought you were very
handsome, but that the likelihood was your wife was
in the ladies room, and that no one as good looking
and professional as you would be single, let alone nice
and charming and sexy and available. Actually I was
so hurting that I did not know just what I wanted...
not a clue, until you spoke your first words to me and
smiled. I melted like a schoolgirl, so desperate was I
to feel good about something, anything at all to take
my mind off my problems and unsure future. And now
look at us....driving in Dallas to an exclusive rooftop
social club to celebrate the start of a totally new career
and life together. What a season this has been!"

I kissed her again as we parked and entered the eleva-
tor to the top floor of the building where the City Club

was located. At the reception desk, the hostess said, "Ms. Lewis and guest, is that correct? Please follow me to our private Executive Dining Room. And may I add my congratulations to you on your new job?"

"My, but word travels fast in this town!" Cathy said with a laugh.

We entered a lovely corner dining room overlooking the city on a beautiful afternoon. The artwork on the walls, the table setting, china, utensils, and stemware were as elegant as any old English men's club in London or Singapore. After meeting all the board members and having a cocktail, we began our luncheon of peppercorn glazed filets, cooked to a perfectly medium rare state. I asked for the privilege of ordering champagne for the twelve of us. When it came, I held my glass high and proposed a toast with General Reardon and the board president's permission. "Gentlemen, from what I know of this lady's talents and history, you have concluded a most successful search in the hiring of C.S. Lewis. May it be a long and fruitful marriage of talents and needs!"

Bruce Cannon, the board President said, "Cathy, this is your club, where you can wine and dine prospective advertisers, and negotiate supplier contracts and other things that may be needed in the coming months. Welcome aboard. We all are expecting great things from you."

So concluded the first big event in Dallas for our future. Cathy was never happier than right now, she told me. So much to look forward to in the coming days... fun and big challenges at the same time.

CHAPTER 14

⚘

Today had gone smoothly so far. We had arrived at DFW with time to spare in the damned inconvenience of our modern airport security procedures, but at last we were on our way to Baltimore and on to Annapolis for the week's festivities surrounding Francis' graduation.

The first words out of Cathy's mouth after we had been served our breakfast aboard the plane was, "Bret, Darling, normally I am calm and unruffled in all situations, but I'm confessing my nervousness about this weekend. You've put together a potentially explosive group of people when the situation calls for love, pride, and peace. I do not see the upside for this grouping you've invited. Would you care to attempt to allay my fears?"

"Okay, here goes, my Love. It's never right to do wrong, but I also think it is never wrong to do the right thing. The right thing in my mind is to go forward, closing some doors while opening others. Let's look at the list of people attending Francis' June Week celebration. I, of course along with his mother Ellen are necessary. Next I see this week as the perfect time for you to be introduced to Francis; you will, after all, soon become his step-Mother, and with the excitement of this culmination of his formal education, and time in the cottage to kick back – we can all just relax and get to know one another. Next is Lori; I like Lori.....I like her a lot, and I know my son. He's a lot like me, and at the very least, he'll feel just that much more important to have a lovely woman his own age to show around the Yard at the Academy, especially a woman whose grandfather was a Captain of one of our nation's battleships. Cathy, I am not at all trying to play matchmaker, but Lori will be part of the new family we are putting together, and I'm certain they will get along well, forming a good friendship, if nothing else. So far I do not see any potential fisticuffs, do you?"

"Maybe not yet, but you are not through the list, Bret."

"Right. I do not hate or even dislike Ellen. I can only wish her well as her life progresses, single or married. So that brings us to Richard. Would you not agree that he is usually a gentleman, and that he loves Lori just about more than anything?

"Yes, but...."

"Now just a minute, let me finish. I know that Richard is driven professionally, and that he has some sort of sex drive because of the behavior that caused him the loss of you in his life. Ellen too is smart, congenial, sexy, and has always wanted to be married to a lawyer, like her mother and grandmother before her. So the only face that would not normally be with us in Annapolis is Richard, correct?

"Okay, go on, Mr. Feelgood."

"In Denver after Lori's graduation dinner at the steakhouse, Richard admitted to me that he was glad you had found someone like me to take care of you, and... here's the important part...that he too would like to find someone. At that time I broached the subject of Ellen without telling him who Ellen was, only that I saw a potential between the two of them and could I mention his name to my 'friend' Ellen? Cathy, he said yes to my idea. So, there will be a lot of exciting things to stimulate us all. Richard will be on good behavior around his precious Lori. Lori will enjoy Francis; and Ellen, not wanting to be left out, will participate fully in our collective activities. Cathy, I'm thinking Commissioning Week just might become a love fest as good as April in Paris!"

"Bret, I guess that's what I like about you. You are a happy man, and determined to spread your happiness everywhere you go."

"Cathy, what's the worst that can happen? Whatever it is, it probably isn't going to come into play, and if it does, we'll deal with it as the resident mature adults, okay?"

"You do seem determined to make it all work. I guess the least I can do is help, so okay, I'm on-board with your plans."

I leaned over and kissed her. "Thanks, Cathy, you're the best!"

Our flight was landing in Baltimore. I had told Cathy about my trip to Annapolis when I began to get the idea of wanting to go to the Academy. That trip was with Mom and Dad back in the early '60's. We had landed at Friendship Airport, the old name for Baltimore's airport.

Today we were landing at BWI on a beautiful day with just a few clouds breaking the sky. We rented a large SUV for the weekend to carry all six of us around during the weekend's festivities and headed straight to the Edgewater cottage I had arranged for three years ago in order to get the property for this time of the year. As we were driving through Annapolis toward the cottage, I asked Cathy about her history with Annapolis. "Father took me when I was a young girl, probably about 12 years old. That has been my only visit, but I remember it was a lovely old historic town."

As we walked inside the rented cottage, Cathy whistled, "Oh, Bret, this is perfect!" She ran to the back of the cottage to take a look at the water view, and was again astounded. "This has to be the best place in all the area," she announced as she walked out onto the lawn which sloped down to the water and the pier.

I was curious if the kayaks I had rented had been delivered yet. They were there, tied alongside the boathouse – three double seat kayaks.

"Bret, I haven't been in a canoe or kayak since I was at Girl Scout camp many, many years ago. Let's get into our swimsuits and go for an outing on the bay."

"Okay, my Dear. You will need a suit. These folks here are somewhat stuffy about middle-aged women bearing it all and sailing in the buff," I said with a laugh. Come inside and let me show you around the place. Inside, I put some music on...Big Band stuff... grabbed Cathy and danced her around the entire verandah, then picked her up and carried her to the master suite.

"Bret, you are a fun guy! Every time we are together, I fall in love with you all over again. I am yours to do with as you please."

"Well, okay then! Here's my plan for the afternoon... make love, go for a boat ride, and then paddle over to one of the waterside seafood restaurants in town."

"Yes! This is going to be a great weekend, Bret!"

"I think so too, even with Richard here."

"Well, that thought makes me a little queasy still, but maybe Lori, Francis, and maybe Ellen can get him to enjoy himself and leave us alone."

"Cathy, I think we all will get along famously, so long as everyone remembers the weekend is all about Francis' graduation and commissioning."

"Bret, come here and let's get started on your afternoon list. I won't ask you, but I have never made love in Maryland before. She smiled her irrestible way, and we were drawn almost immediately into another period of intimacy that was off the charts for our feelings and emotions for each other.

Down at the pier waterside, I gave Cathy some rudimentary tips on boat handling for our afternoon kayak journey into town. The afternoon was serenely calm and warm, the water smooth. "We're likely to work up a sweat paddling over to the Crab House at the Annapolis Dock," I said "but they have some ice cold beer on tap to go with their hard-shell crabs."

"Let's go, Bret. It's been years since I've enjoyed fresh crabs right on the water."

The excursion, although a little over three miles of paddling one way, was thoroughly pleasant. We took our time, watching the shore birds and ducks, who were as curious about us as we were of them. I remembered that I had not yet called Francis to let him know we were in town a day earlier than originally planned. When I texted him we were in town, my cell phone went off within three minutes. "Great, Dad!" Francis exclaimed. "Where are you and when do I get to meet Cathy?"

"Francis, I'll let Cathy answer those questions," I said handing the telephone to Cathy.

"Ms. Lewis, I can't believe the day is finally here that I am going to get to meet you – the woman who has made my father come alive again! Where are you both?"

"Francis, we are actually in a kayak out on the bay heading toward some crab house at the Annapolis City Dock. And Francis, please call me Cathy."

"Okay then. Cathy, I know the place you're headed toward, and if it's alright, I will be there saving a table outside for the three of us. I am really looking forward to meeting you!"

Cathy handed me the phone. "Well, Francis, in the words of Admiral Farragut at Mobile Bay, 'Damn the torpedoes, full speed ahead' – can you meet us at the dock?"

"Dad, I'll be there holding a waterside table before the two of you to arrive. Good-bye Dad, and I am really looking forward to meeting Cathy."

"Bret, he sounds so much like a young version of you. I know that I am going to love him as if he were my own child."

"Oh, Cathy, I hope that is true. Until I met you, Francis was the only thing in my life that mattered at all.

And now I am going to have a family again – the four of us exploring a new world together."

"You really think Francis and Lori will get along without a lot of sibling rivalries? I mean you are the only one who has a knowledge of both of them at this point."

"Cathy, I'm certain of it. Remember that Francis is more like me than Ellen. He's extroverted, passionate about everything in life, and very optimistic. And he likes a pretty woman. He and Lori may have five minutes of uncertainty seeing both their mother and their father around other people, but soon they will be off learning about each other as potential step-siblings. I just see it as one of the truly great weekends ever for all of us."

"Bret, you are the only man who could make me feel comfortable at a moment like this. I guess I will have to trust you some more, and be glad you are the way you are. I mean, your lows are higher than other people's highs – you are a truly amazing man, Bret."

At that precise moment, Cathy looked up toward the restaurant at the dock and noticed a midshipman in his whites standing at the rail and taking a photograph of the two of us and our kayak approaching the restaurant. "That must be Francis," Cathy said, noticing that I was all smiles, and waving my paddle in the air like a teenager myself.

We tied up dockside as the handsome Brigade six-stripper leaned forward and took Cathy's hand, helping her up and out of the kayak. "Cathy, you are good for Dad. He would never be on the water today were it not for you. The sun and salt air is good for the both of you. My name is Francis Bret Harte, Jr., and you, I am certain are the beautiful C.S. Lewis, the woman who has totally captivated my father. I am so very pleased to meet you, and Dad, I am so glad you are here. There's so much we have to talk about and so little time!"

"Well, Francis, you took the words right out of my mouth! So was I right in my descriptions of Cathy?"

"Well, not exactly, Dad. You could have just said she looks like Miss America of 1990 or later."

"Francis, I can see you running for Commander-in-Chief even before you make Admiral with a line like that, ha!"

"Francis, the really good news is that Cathy has a single daughter every bit as pretty and charming as herself who's coming here soon, and that if you play your cards right, Cathy will allow you to be her escort for the next few days. Every Brigade Commander needs to have a beautiful blonde at his side for June Week festivities, right Son?"

"Well, Mrs. Lewis,...Cathy, I am an officer and a gentleman. Do you think you can convince your Lori to dance with me at the Officer's Club Friday night?"

"Francis, I will put in a good word, but you will have to do the selling. It shouldn't be too hard because she adored her grandfather, Captain Schuyler, Class of 1940."

"You both must be tired. Let's get a cold drink and some crabs. Do you like hard-shell crabs, Cathy?"

"I certainly do, Francis!"

"After this week's menu of crabs, crab chowder, crab cakes, crab stew, crab bisque, and crab salad, you will be ready for some Texas barbecue, right Dad?"

We all laughed. It seemed things were going well with the first introduction of Cathy to my son.

"Francis, seriously....all those stripes on your shoulder boards.... are you a cadet admiral or something?" Cathy asked, clearly curious about the impressive insignia Francis was wearing.

"Not quite, Cathy. I was selected as the Brigade Commander for the spring semester. I have two regimental commanders under me; they each wear five stripes. They are good friends of mine; you will get to meet them at the Admiral's dinner Thursday night. Dad, we have a new Superintendent, a really neat guy, a Vice-Admiral out of the Pentagon. He asked to meet you Thursday. Can I assume that you, Cathy, and Lori will be able to attend the special dinner at the Superintendent's Quarters Thursday?"

"I suppose so Francis. I am not accustomed to saying 'No' to an Admiral ever."

We continued our lunch with me, the proud Father, and Cathy too enjoying everything about the afternoon.

Cathy excused herself to take a telephone call. When she
returned, it was to announce that Lori had just landed at
BWI airport, and could we go out to pick her up?

Francis took charge. "Yes," he said. "Here's the plan
I suggest. We'll leave the kayak tied up here at the Crab
House. Phil, the restaurant manager will watch it for us.
We'll head out to BWI, pick up Lori, the special guest of
honor, and return here to the restaurant. Dad, you and
Cathy can return to the cottage in my car, and if Lori's
willing, she and I will paddle the kayak back to Edgewater
Shores and the cottage. That way Lori and I can become
acquainted, and we can have some lemonade or some-
thing stronger, if required once we arrive at the cottage."

"Lori will love that, Francis. Let's be off."

Aside to Francis as we waited for the valet to bring up
his car, I said, "Son, thanks for being such a good sport
about this strange turn in your June Week activities. I'm
certain you will have a great time — we all will. We will
not be strangers long. Lori looks like her Mom, has just
graduated from the University of Denver, and is totally
unattached, so I think the two of you can have some
fun together this weekend. She's still hurting just a bit
about her father Richard losing her mother, but she has
decided she likes me, and that we can all probably get
along for the long haul. Just be kind to her and show
her a good time, alright, Son?"

"Dad, you leave it to me. She'll have the best time of
her life. I mean, after all, she's going to be kin to me
someday, right?"

"Yes, that is a given, Francis!"

We went into the terminal baggage claim area, all three of us, looking for Lori. No problem finding her; she was sitting atop her luggage, cell phone in hand, checking her messages. Lori looked up and shrieked, "Wow, that was fast! What kind of rocketship are you flying?" she said with her mother's gleam in her eyes. Hugging her mother and paying her respects to me, Lori then turned to the one of us who looked official and not at all like a tourist and said, "You must be Ensign Harte!"

No, fair lady, today I am Midshipman Brigade Commander Francis Harte, but by Saturday afternoon, you will be right, I'll just be another freshly commissioned Ensign. But I am very glad to meet you, Sis!"

Although surprised, Lori was quick on her feet, "If a girl has to have a step-brother late in life, he might as well be handsome. Good job picking him, Mom!" We all laughed. It looked to me as though things were going to be just fine.

"Lori, you are going to love the cottage Bret and Francis have picked out. We only arrived earlier this morning, and have already had our fill of crab cakes for lunch," Cathy told her daughter after we had fitted us all and Lori's baggage into Francis' car.

"This is a really cool rental car," Lori said.

"Actually, it's my graduation present from Dad," Francis said beamingly. He definitely liked the fact that Lori had noticed.

"Can we pick up my Dad tomorrow in it, Francis? He's scheduled to arrive in the early afternoon on Wednesday."

"Sure thing, Lori. I am looking forward to meeting him. He's an attorney, isn't he? I'll make this suggestion....Mom is coming in from South Carolina around 15:30 hours, excuse me....that's 3:30 p.m. tomorrow. Maybe we can pick both of them up at the same time and save some driving. Neither of them should have to take a cab."

"Oh, Francis, that'll be perfect!" Lori said with clear excitement in her response. "Does that sound okay with you, Mom?"

"Lori, Bret and I will be getting the clambake ready at the cottage. Can I count on you and Francis to take care of retrieving the new arrivals?" Cathy asked as she winked at me.

"We can do that, right Francis?....please?"

"Now, Dad, who can resist a request coming from not one, but two beautiful women?"

"Francis, it's always going to be a problem. We men just have to learn to deal with it," I said with a big grin on my face. Now for the immediate problem facing us with the car and kayak....what's your suggestion again?"

In answer, Francis said, "Lori, Cathy and Dad paddled a kayak over to the City Dock Crab House where I met them for lunch. They need to get back to the cottage, so I thought they could use my car while we take the kayak back to the cottage. Can I count on you to do some of the paddling?"

"Francis, that sounds fun to me. Can I change clothes at the restaurant?"

"Yes, I need to get out of my whites also and into some shorts."

In the back seat, I wrote Cathy a note, "See, no problem, ha!" Cathy winked back her quite happy acknowledgement.

Back at the restaurant, Lori found some clothes in her overnight bag to change into. Once they were standing on the dock ready to begin their trip to the cottage, I said to Francis, "If you run into a tsunami or a Chesapeake Loch Ness monster, be sure you save Lori, okay? You will need her to put on your new shoulder boards on Saturday – I may be too choked up Son to do it alone. You know how sentimental I am."

With a laugh, Francis said, "Cathy, I am so glad you are here to take care of my overly maudlin Father. We all will be cool and calm; it's Dad I am worried about!"

"I'm with your father, Francis. Some day you, too, will have a son or daughter making you proud, and I'm here to tell you, it's a very happy moment."

Cathy and I watched as Francis helped Lori into her front seat of the kayak. Cathy yelled out, "That's my water bottle in the front pocket, if you need it." In just seconds they were away and headed out into the bay and down to Edgewater on the other side of Eastport. Cathy said, "Bret, you may want a photo of this moment – our children paddling so carefree together on their first day of meeting. I so hope they enjoy this week like we will. Bret, I am so happy at this moment."

I pulled her close and kissed her. "Me too, Darling."

CHAPTER 15

Cathy and I arrived back at the Edgewater cottage and began the unpacking we should have done when we first landed. There were three bedrooms along with a study which had a sofa fold-out bed. Cathy picked the upstairs bedroom for us because of the attached bath and the stunning view out over the bay from the small upstairs deck. She suggested that Lori could have the downstairs guest room just off the verandah with its separate entrance. Francis would likely want to stay with us for an evening or two between his duties at the Academy directing the final activities of the year for both regiments of the brigade he commanded. I was proud of him, to say the very least.

By the time we had completed our unpacking and getting our grocery list together, we heard laughing down at the pier and boat dock. "That's a good sign," I said. "They seem to be enjoying each other's company."

"Bret, Darling, Lori is ready for a romance, perhaps too ready. I hope you will caution Francis to take it easy with her. He is, after all, one handsome young man, and in uniform, he cuts a striking figure. What woman would not be bowled over?"

"Cathy, I will check out his feelings and actions. He is not a cad or womanizer. For all her faults, Ellen taught him good manners and respect for women. I just want them to have a good time together, but I am beginning to think already that they will not have a normal step brother, step sister relationship."

"Oh, gosh, Bret, I have not even thought about the possibility of a romance between the two of them. Whatever would we do if that happened?"

"Not a thing! That would be funny though, wouldn't it?"

"Too weird to even think about, Bret!"

"I am most concerned about Richard. Ellen has a reason to be here to see her son graduate. I am hoping that Richard does not feel like a fifth wheel and out of place in all the festivities. The very best thing would be for he and Ellen to hit it off, don't you think?"

"Bret, it's all surreal to me. Just thinking about Richard being here around us for a weekend together sort of gives me a certain unease."

"We'll see. Let's keep an open mind and hope for the best – that Ellen will not dislike you and that Richard will find some attractive features about Ellen. Now let's go down to the pier and see what adventure the kids had getting here from downtown Annapolis."

"Well, Lori, did my son command the boat and voyage safely? No capsizes, right?"

"He did well, Bret. We took a slight detour so Francis could point out some rather interesting history about the American Revolution involving Lafayette and General Washington. He hasn't yet mentioned his historical tour fee for the ride, ha."

"Come on inside the house. Cathy has some lemonade made. We can sit on the porch and make some plans for the rest of the weekend. Francis, do you have an itinerary for all the things that are scheduled for the rest of the week?"

"You bet, Dad! I'll lay it all out up at the house. You and Cathy didn't put any scratches on my new car, did you?"

"Nope! We didn't even get it over 40 mph coming out to the cottage."

As we assembled on the verandah, I was amused watching Francis demonstrate his impeccable manners, pulling out Cathy's chair, and positioning Lori next to her, but very close to him also. It was pleasantly clear that Francis was not only comfortable with the women, but very interested in their liking him also.

Francis pulled out his events schedule. "The first thing on the calendar for us all is the Superintendant's Dinner. We have a new Admiral in charge since last August. He is well liked, and a strong leader for the Academy. As Midshipman Brigade Commander, I have been in a number of meetings with him this spring. He wants to meet you Dad! I have a table for up to six guests right next to his for tomorrow's dinner honoring all the Brigade staff for the year. His wife is a real asset to his career; she's from Pittsburgh, so Cathy, I'm betting you and she will have some things to talk about."

"Is the dinner in the Mess Hall?"

"No Dad, it's smaller than that with more time to actually visit with the Admiral, the Commandant, and their immediate staffs. The dinner is in the Supt's quarters right next to the chapel. The new Superintendant was in the Class of '74, six years before you, Dad."

"So who's on your list of six to go to the dinner, Francis?"

"Well, the four of us, and Mom, of course. Lori, I'm hoping that Mr. Lewis, your father can join us. Would that be okay with everyone? Cathy?"

"Francis, it's your week! I am here to see and enjoy everything. If you can get Lori to sell Richard on the idea, I will be on my best behavior for you," Cathy said with a degree of incredulity in her response.

"Then it's done. I will turn in those names for the place cards at dinner. We all will be in diner dress white uniforms — dinner or cocktail dresses for the women and dark suits for the men. Dad, not your plaid golf blazer, okay?" Francis said kiddingly.

"Francis, can you stay and have dinner with the three of us tonight?"

"I thought you might never ask, Dad?"

"Well, I did bring a special bottle of wine all the way from Texas to go with our steaks tonight in your honor. First thing I need to do is get to the market for some groceries. Cathy, do you have the list for me and Francis?"

"Yes, upstairs, Can you join me for a minute?"

"Lori, you can get Francis to show you around the cottage. This is the second time we've stayed here over the last few years – it's our favorite of all the summer rentals. Francis, I'll be down in a few minutes to head out with you to the store."

Upstairs, Cathy embraced me warmly. "Here's the grocery list, my darling man. Bret, although I am somewhat apprehensive about seeing Richard tomorrow and meeting Ellen for the first time, this afternoon and evening I am so at peace and hopeful. Everything is just beautiful. Our two children are radiantly happy and enjoying each other, the weather is perfect, you're perfect, and I am happier that I can remember. Kiss me and tell me that I am not dreaming, will you?"

"Cathy, it is good to be alive! That's what I believe today at this very moment. You and Lori settle in; we'll be back in an hour or less to begin dinner, firing up the outdoor grill for the best cuts of beef I can find at whatever store Francis drives me to."

Coming down the stairs, I found Francis and Lori dancing on the verandah to some soft music playing on the sound system. "Bret, you never warned me about how romantic my blind date would be!" Lori was clearly under the spell cast by Francis.

"Lori, do you want me to call him off? Annapolis men do tend to get a bit aggressive in the spring when placed in the company of beautiful women."

"Please don't, Bret. I am enjoying every minute of this! My Mom's having fun; I want to also."

"Good, Lori. I make a very poor chaperone anyway?"

"Ready, Francis, to pick out some good steaks for us tonight?" And we left for the market.

When Francis and I returned from grocery shopping, the sun was low in the sky, foretelling a beautiful sunset ahead. We came inside to a dining room of wonderful fragrance from fresh cut flowers the women had gathered from the beds outside coupled with some scented candles that Cathy had going in several spots around the cottage. Pointing to the porch I suggested, "Why don't you and Lori go out and plan tomorrow's activities as I pour us some drinks and get the steaks ready to grill? Lori, what is your preference for a drink before dinner?"

Lori was her mother's daughter – "I'll have a glass of white wine, please."

"May I, Dad?" Francis asked as he poured himself a glass from a new bottle of 15 year old Glenmorangie, and took Lori her wine out to the porch swing.

"Have I told you how much I enjoy cooking with you?" was the response from Cathy as I set down her glass of wine in the kitchen.

"That's my line," I said with a smile. "It is a very special evening Cathy – better than I could have dreamed up just a year ago. It's so good to see Francis as happy and animated as he is with Lori. I was hoping, but could not have guessed it might go this well for the two of them. Did Lori indicate she was having a good time to you while we were out buying groceries?"

"Bret, she confided a bunch of feelings to me, all positive. I'll tell you about our conversation tonight later when we are in bed. I think even you might be surprised."

"Now that's something to look forward to, Cathy. Can we be ready to eat in 20 minutes or so? I'm ready to put the steaks on the grill."

"Yes, do it!"

"Lori, your rib eye is to be cooked medium rare, right?"

"Yes, how did you know that?"

"Well, as the second most important woman in my life, I took notice how you ordered your steak at the steakhouse in Denver for your graduation dinner. Francis, you should have been there! We had fun didn't we, Lori?"

"Bret, you know I love my Daddy, but given everything that's happened over the last year, I guess I have to confess that I am glad Mother found you over in Ireland last fall. I mean, look at us tonight – none of this would be happening if Mom hadn't gone to Ireland to find herself. At least I wouldn't be here on the East Coast in the company of a handsome young naval officer, attending garden parties, and boating on the Chesapeake.... none of that without Mom getting you to her table in the dining room at Craggy Rock Lodge!"

"Lori, you make it sound like I was prowling and on the make in Ireland for an affair. That is not at all what happened!"

"Mom, it's okay. Everybody's happy here tonight, right Bret and Francis?"

"Let's all drink to that," I said. "You two might wish to wash up for dinner. The steaks will be on the table in less than five minutes."

Dinner was animated with laughter and participation from all of us about the events of the last twelve months, Lori telling about her ski trip with a guy who turned out to be a 'mama's boy' back in the late winter, and Francis describing his adventures in Puerto Rico on his summer cruise last year. It was good for Cathy and me to sit back and listen to our separate offspring tell of their experiences, and laugh at themselves for their embarrassing gaffs at times. Clearly they both were enjoying each other's stories.

"Francis, are you staying here tonight?" I asked as we were finishing our coffee and dessert.

"Dad, I have some things I have to attend to back at Mother Bancroft early tomorrow, but after that I would like to be here with you all for the rest of the week, okay?"

"Mother Bancroft?" Lori queried of Francis.

"Yeah, that's our description of the world's largest dormitory, Bancroft Hall. I am right in the middle in the 17th Company. When Dad was here, there were 36 companies; today there's only 30, divided into two regiments of three battalions each."

"Wow, that's a lot more confusing than sororities and fraternities, Francis."

Francis smiled. "I should be going, but I will wake you guys up for coffee and breakfast early tomorrow if that's okay...say 07:30 or so?" With that, Francis took his cover (his combination cap or hat), reached over to Lori, and kissed her good-night.

"Hey, Midshipman, come back here and do that again a little slower."

For the first time in years, I saw Francis act surprised. But, he recovered his poise quickly, threw his cap on the floor, grabbed Lori, and gave her an embrace and kiss like he had been at sea for two months straight.

"Well, sailor, I will be up early in the morning and have your coffee waiting....don't be late!"

Francis picked up his cap, winked at me, and left with a huge smile embossed across his face.

"Tell you girls what. I am a happy man tonight. You both can go for a night stroll on the beach, and I will clean up the dinner dishes, and have a cigar and my coffee on the verandah until you return."

Cathy looked at Lori. "Sounds good to me. You ready to go?"

What a great first day this had been in Annapolis. I tried to remember my June Week thirty years ago. It was all fuzzy; the memories were not as good as the feelings I was holding inside just now. And the week/weekend was just beginning!

CHAPTER 16

I awoke in the morning to the smell of coffee brewing, always a great way to start the day if someone else has gotten up early to start the coffee pot. Someone had; it was Lori. Cathy and I came down the stairs with sleep still in our eyes. Lori, on the other hand, was dressed and looking terrific for a day of sightseeing, meeting Francis' mom, Ellen, and reuniting with her father, Richard.

"Good morning, you two! It's another beautiful day; I hiked down to the market for a newspaper – the birds are out and flowers are blooming – it's just great outside."

Cathy looked my way and smiled. She, as I, liked seeing her Lori excited and happy.

As she was pouring my coffee, Lori asked, "Bret, I haven't confirmed anything with Francis yet about today, but I would really like to have that tour you promised me in Denver of old town Annapolis and the Yard at the Academy. Could we squeeze some sightseeing in before Francis and I would have to be on the way to the airport to pick up our other guests?"

"I think so. Cathy, you okay with a trip around some neat history?"

"What choice do I have? It looks to me like you two have decided, but just to keep it a unanimous family decision, I'm onboard!"

About that instant, Francis came into the kitchen breakfast area. "Okay, what have I missed so far?"

"Well, Son, I know you are ready to take on your leadership role as an officer, but we three have pulled rank on you and decided to weigh anchor on an official historical tour of Annapolis forthwith! Are you onboard with that?"

"Great idea! We have just about enough time before Lori and I need to be at BWI to pick up Mom and her dad. Any coffee left, Lori?"

While Lori and Francis visited over their coffee and muffins, Cathy and I hurried upstairs to shower and dress for the morning's activities. "The two of them are getting along way better than I had even hoped. Should I be worried?" Cathy asked in the vein of all mothers' concerns, I guess.

"Cathy, they are adults now, and we have to allow them to make their own decisions in life from this point forward. Of course, I would hope they would have the common sense to ask for advice before leaping off any bridges."

"Oh, Bret, I am just being protective of my only hatchling. I was worried she might not have a good time, and now I am worried she will be having too much fun, so much so that her judgment might be clouded."

"And your concern is.....?"

"Francis is so good looking, poised, and professional that I fear he may have a number of hearts to break before he finds the right girl for him for the long haul."

"Cathy, Francis is not like most sailors. He is a tender, caring, devoted Christian man with a bright future. He will need someone like Lori to pull off a very successful career in the Navy or outside it. I will be happy if they continue and develop as a couple. If not, they will likely always be good friends because of you and me. Darling, please do not concern yourself with any negative consequences down the road. God, for some reason, is smiling on us and our children."

"And our Ex's?" Cathy shot back.

"I'm not touching that subject. They are on their own, but with my blessings on whatever happens to them, except some catastrophe, of course."

"Bret, you are so calm; you are also right, probably."

"Probably? Let's get downstairs and get that tour started."

As we drove into the downtown area, I was surprised at how many buildings and sites Francis could point out and comment on as to what some founding father did 250 years ago. It was fun to see how his love of history had followed mine. We parked on State Circle and began to take in all the beauty and history connected to the very spot we stood.

"Guys, on my first trip here with my Mom and Dad back when I was still in grade school; we all stopped to look at all the commotion going on right here at this stop sign where Francis Street intersects State Circle. How little did I realize that 40 some years later, I would be standing here again with my own son and that he would be named Francis. What happened that summer night in 1968," I said pointing toward the front doors of the Statehouse, "was some political history being made right in front of us. Richard and Pat Nixon came out in the company of Spiro Agnew from his office inside. In those days, security was incredibly lax by today's standards at least. Mr. Nixon and his wife got into their limo just a few feet away from us; I could have touched either of them without much difficulty. Photographers and video cameras were recording it all. The next morning we read the front page headlines in 'The Baltimore Sun', 'Nixon Picks Governor Agnew for His Running Mate'."

"Wow, Dad, you never told me that story."

"Francis, when I write the family history, you will find out a lot of things that you and I never had a chance to talk about. It was my fault for being away for much of your growing up years. I really hope to make it up to you now as I face my retirement years with plenty of time on my hands."

"Not too much spare time, Bret," Cathy interjected. "With my new job, you are going to be escorting me all over the world as I write about senior living and travel!"

We went inside the State House and the old Senate Chamber where Francis was eagerly waiting to tell Lori and Cathy about General Washington surrendering his sword as Commander-in-Chief of the Revolutionary

Army in 1783 in that very room. Out in the rotunda, Francis continued telling us about the Maryland State House being the oldest capitol still in use, the only one that ever served as our nation's capital, and how the dome is the largest wooden one in the world to be constructed without any nails.

At lunchtime, we opted to dine outside at one of the restaurants that looked out onto the Statehouse lawn. From our table we had a clear view of the historic Statehouse and its grounds. As we waited for our lunch, Francis continued his history lesson, clearly enjoying his role. "In 1783 Benjamin Franklin returned with the Treaty of Paris ending the Revolutionary War. It still needed to be ratified by the new Congress of the United States. They met right here in that building; the Statehouse was serving as the capitol of the new republic. Once the ratification ceremonies were completed, two of the delegates, Thomas Jefferson and James Madison climbed up the stairs and went out onto the catwalk right up there and stayed for half an hour together watching the sun set over the harbor. When they came down, someone asked them what the view was like from up there. James Madison said, "There is not a more comely view in all America than the view from there of Annapolis and its harbor at sunset."

Lori was thrilled. "You mean that two of our founding fathers, Jefferson and Madison, walked right there?" she said pointing to the dome walkway.

"Yes, Lori. All of them were right here over 225 years ago. Annapolis is an interesting place, huh?"

We all were enjoying our lunch of Maryland crab cakes and chowder. Looking at his watch, Francis suggested that it was nearing time for he and Lori to start heading for the airport to meet both Richard and Ellen who were coming in on separate flights from San Francisco and Columbia, SC. I paid the check while

Francis supervised getting the women loaded. Since our car was back at the cottage, Francis and Lori agreed to drop us back there and then continue on to BWI. Both the kids seemed excited at seeing their other parent halves, Lori's father and Francis' mother. I asked if they were comfortable introducing Richard and Ellen and explaining the rather unique nature of this weekend's gathering. Francis was completely upbeat, "Dad, I think it's wonderful that everyone significant is going to be here for my graduation and commissioning. Although I do not know Mr. Lewis, I am looking forward to meeting him and am willing to bet that he will like Mother."

"Okay, I am depending on you two to help smooth what could be some difficult feelings having the 'ex's' in the midst of this weekend's festivities. And I very much desire Richard to be made to feel welcomed and a part of everything, not just a fifth wheel outsider looking in on our fun. Can you both help accomplish that early on at the airport meeting? Lori?...and Francis?"

"Dad, I know how uncomfortable this whole thing might be for you and Cathy, BUT I promise to help out in doing exactly what you have asked. Mom wants and deserves to participate fully. I am so lucky to have both of you here. You and Cathy are having fun. Lori and I are enjoying each other too, and I promise to go overboard in my making both the new guests feel completely comfortable."

"Me too, Bret and Mom! Dad is going to enjoy himself; I'll see to that. Wouldn't it be wonderful if he and Ellen hit it off?"

"That would almost be asking too much! But it would be something, wouldn't it?" I replied back to Lori. The kids dropped us at the cottage and headed for the Baltimore airport. "What a nice morning it was," I said to Cathy.

"Would you like to make it a better afternoon, Bret?"

"I thought you might never ask!"

CHAPTER 17

F rancis and Lori arrived at BWI in time to position themselves at the claim area where Richard's
bags would arrive. "Are you excited Lori to see
your father?" Francis asked.

"Yes, we have a wonderful relationship, Francis. He is
still hurting from the divorce, and I am a little surprised
he agreed to Bret's invitation to come to Annapolis. We
all had such a good time at my graduation. Francis, your
father is such a softie. I mean he could see how Dad was
hurting, and in his goodness of heart, maybe not the
wisest thing, but still he asked Richard to be part of June
Week with all of us. I think he has some notion of being
a matchmaker between Richard and Ellen. Would that
be too weird?"

"Weird? Over the top weird! But my mom is a nice
person and deserves a good man in her life. She just
has made no effort whatever to meet anyone since she
and Dad split when I was little. Mom came from a line

of lawyers. She used to ask Bret why he wouldn't go to law school and was mad that he decided against studying law. So Richard's being an attorney by profession is a possible plus when they meet. Mom knows about you, but nothing of Richard. I do not think she has a clue that Bret is thinking of her as a date for Richard this weekend. Let's you and I help make them comfortable together by asking them to dinner one evening, just the four of us. What do you think?"

"Sure, Francis, if you would like to. That might in fact be a good way to get the ice melted! Here he comes – that man in the camel blazer is my father," Lori shrieked as she ran to hug Richard.

"How's my number one favorite woman in the world?" Richard asked.

"Oh, Father, I am just great, having the time of my life. And may I introduce a gentleman who is largely responsible for showing me such a good time? Father, this is Francis Harte, Jr., soon to be Ensign Francis Harte. Francis, this great man is my Dad, Richard Lewis."

Francis was very gracious in acknowledging and welcoming Richard to Maryland. "Mr. Lewis, allow me to carry your bags to the car while you and Lori visit together."

"Okay, Francis, but please call me Richard, if you do not mind."

Francis carried Richard's bags to the car outside the terminal building while Lori visited with her dad and explained that we all would be meeting Francis' mother, Ellen, who was also arriving shortly from Columbia, SC.

When Francis came back from the car, he suggested that they have a drink in one of the airport lounges until Ellen's flight arrived in less than an hour. Once seated, Richard looking at Francis, asked, "So this Ellen that Bret mentioned to me in Denver at Lori's graduation.... she is actually your mom, Francis?"

"Yes, Richard, I guess so."

"Are you two close? When was the last time you got to see her before today?" Richard asked, clearly curious.

"Yes, Richard, very close like you and Lori. My father was away on sea duty a lot when I was young, so Mom had to fill in as both Father, disciplinarian, and Mother, all at the same time. She's a neat lady in many ways. She came up last fall to the Duke football weekend and Homecoming – she was my date, ha! And, I saw her over Christmas leave."

"Well, I am looking forward to meeting her and to the entire weekend. Shouldn't I get a rental car, Francis?"

"We have two cars already, Richard. We all will be together for most of the functions of the weekend, so I do not see the need for that expense. But if you would feel more comfortable having one to come and go from your B&B, I can drop you anytime at one of the downtown car rental locations."

"Good. Then we will play it by ear. Where am I staying? Bret said on the telephone last week that he had taken care of the reservation for me."

"Actually we were very lucky to get both you and Mom rooms at one of the best places in town over at the Eastport House. It is the oldest house in Eastport, once the best and closest village to Annapolis, just across Spa Creek from the old historic downtown dock area. It's walking distance to Gate One at the Academy. As you might imagine, the entire area east of Washington and south of Baltimore is filled to capacity with families and friends for Commissioning Week Festivities. I hope you like seafood, especially crab."

"Well, Francis, that all sounds just great. And I do enjoy seafood. We get mostly Dungeness crab out on the West Coast; I am looking forward to trying some Maryland Blue Hard-shell Crab."

"Lori, I can see your father has done his homework. Why am I not surprised? Richard, I promise you will get your fill of crab in all its forms this weekend.....crab cakes, crab chowder, crab bisque, and crab omelettes. We'll get started tonight at our June Week cottage with a cookout my father is handling with boiled crabs, his famous crab cakes recipe, and some barbecue brisket Texas style just to keep kosher on his Texas heritage."

"It does sound fun, Lori."

"Just wait 'til you see the cottage, Dad. It's right on the bay with every amenity...very relaxing and the company promises to be good, right Francis?"

"Richard, I hope you and Ellen get along. She is very selective, and so far as I know, has made no efforts in 15 years to find a companion or even a date. So she will likely be a nervous wreck in the presence of so debonair and fashionable a guy as you, Richard."

"Oh, please Francis. I am just a regular guy in need of many of the same things as Ellen likely desires. I'm betting we all have a great time."

"Thanks in advance Richard for your understanding. I am really glad you are here. I very much like your daughter and she will have an even better time now that you are here. Let's get started by heading over to the baggage claim and retrieving Mom, okay?"

"Lori kissed her dad. It's just great you are here; I am so happy now!" Richard for all his faults did love his daughter, and clearly his eyes showed that he, too, was happy, just being here in Lori's presence.

Next came the part we all were concerned about – meeting Ellen and assuming she would be comfortable with having Richard as her unannounced dinner partner for the weekend.

They ambled back toward the baggage claim area where they would meet Ellen once her flight arrived and she deplaned to claim her luggage. Lori continued her animated discussions with Richard about every trivial thing that crossed her mind. Francis was happy too, now knowing the entire family that raised Lori; she seemed a good mix of the two, Richard and Cathy. Sooner than was expected, Ellen came down the stairs to the baggage area. Francis ran over to his Mom, kissed and hugged her, and exclaimed, "Wow, you look terrific, Mom. I want to hear what program you are on, so I can start the same exact regimen!"

"Francis, it's also good to see you, my handsome Navy graduate, but you can stop the flattery – it makes me wonder what you are up to. And now who are these folks you've brought out to the airport?"

"Well, Mom, from our recent conversations, you know the names, and now I will add the faces for you. First, this is Richard Lewis who has also just arrived for the weekend's festivities from San Francisco. Richard, this is my mother, Ellen Harte. And now I'd like you to meet Lori Lewis, Richard's daughter, and a new graduate herself of the University of Denver just two weeks ago."

Richard began his sales campaign immediately, "Francis, you did not tell me your mother was so young and beautiful. Ms. Harte, it's good to meet you."

"And Mr. Lewis, are you in politics in California?" Ellen asked him pointedly.

"No, Mrs. Harte, I am an attorney in private practice," Richard said laughing.

"May I call you Richard?" And I am Ellen, please."

"Ellen it is then. Please allow me to carry your bags to the car so you and Francis can visit together."

The fact that Francis was holding Lori's hand did not escape Ellen's attention. "Francis, it seems that you and Lori are getting along well. Why haven't I heard more about her from you?"

"Mom, I only met Lori yesterday. It appears she is going to be my step-sister soon, so I decided to learn all about her, and so far everything I've learned, I like. This gathering of Dad and Lori's mom and you and Richard this weekend is complicated, and more than just a little unusual. Of course, Dad and I are hoping it all works out that we all can become friends and have a great time together during my Commissioning Week activities. Does that sound too just too cracked and too unrealistic to pull off?"

"Francis, I am not in charge of anything, but if you are asking me if I can get along with you and Lori and Richard this weekend, the answer is 'Yes! I can'. Your new friends seem charming – what's not to like?"

"There, Richard, Mom seems sold. If I can just talk you into being her escort for the upcoming activities, then my duty is completed."

"Francis, don't fret. I am not accustomed to being in the company of so pretty a woman, so I am looking forward to my job of being Ellen's escort if that is your request."

Francis leaned over, kissed Lori, and whispered, "Wow, whoever would have thought that pulling off this grouping amicably would have been this easy? I am happy today! Let's get Richard and Ellen delivered to the Eastport House so we can all begin to relax and get ready for Dad's outdoor feast at the cottage." Lori explained to Richard and Ellen in the backseat the plan for the evening...Hawaiian shirts and shorts for the crab fest at the cottage in Edgewater Estates, about eight miles away by car, but only one mile by water.

"Dad and Ms. Harte, what Francis and I were thinking......"

"Lori, please call me Ellen."

"Certainly, Mrs. Harte, I mean Ellen. What Francis and I were thinking is that we will drop you both at the B&B. While you are getting settled in, we'll go to the market for some items that Bret and Mom need. By the time we've finished our shopping errand, you and Dad should be ready. We'll stop back by and load up for the big feast Bret is preparing for us all."

"And Richard, we have two cars, so you and Mom can take the other auto back here to Eastport whenever you desire tonight. Does that sound alright Mom?"

"That's okay with me if you can show Richard how to get back here," was Ellen's response.

Later after Francis and Lori returned to pick up the new arrivals at the Eastport House and loaded the car for the cottage, Richard and Ellen were asked about their accommodations. Francis was curious since no one, except Ellen, had actually stayed there.

"It's one of the nicest guest houses in Annapolis, "Ellen offered. "Is your room and bath okay, Richard?"

"Quite so, Ellen. I think we will both be very comfortable this weekend."

When the new arrivals landed at the cottage, everyone, both inside the car and in the house, were apprehensive. Cathy had been right weeks earlier in her assessment that the grouping of guests had the potential to be unpleasant, if not downright explosive with the intertwined love relationships and jealousy involved. Within the first five minutes, I did my best to diffuse all uncomfortableness, greeting and embracing our guests, especially Richard, whom I knew would have some problem in his role as an outsider.

Once we all were inside and everyone had a drink in their hand, I asked for a minute to address the obvious – this collection of two different families split and rejoined. "At the start of this weekend celebrating Francis' achievements ...as we did Lori's just a few days ago in Denver, I would like to set the tone for the great weekend ahead. More than most men, I can appreciate the incredible nature of this party, as unusual as any of us will likely ever experience again. Francis has to be here; the rest of us came voluntarily out of a desire to meet and celebrate as best we can. I throw out the challenge to all to endeavor to make it memorable for everyone, especially the youngest members, who I hope can live a long life and be able to recount with fondness the events that took place here in Annapolis in 2010. In hopes that we can put aside differences and begin looking to a glorious future, I propose a toast to Francis in his not so small accomplishments and to Lori. May they both live incredibly successful lives in this great country!"

Everyone lifted their glasses high and drank cheerfully to my toast. Now for the first time in many hours, I, too, began to relax. Feeling this weekend was beginning to look even better than I had hoped, I looked over to Cathy. She was beaming; even Richard seemed okay, and Ellen, the wildcard in this mix, seemed ready to let her hair down and have some fun.

We adjourned outside to the lawn facing the bay. It was a beautifully balmy spring evening just before summer's start. Cathy had helped me get everything ready; I wanted an absolutely perfect first night to set the tone for a truly great weekend for Francis...for us all really. Announcing that dinner was ready, I ladled from a huge kettle the first course – crab bisque, straight from the recipe that Mrs. O'Doyle had given me last Fall in County Galway, Ireland. "This is perfection, Bret."

I looked up to see from whom the comment came, and was shocked! It was actually Ellen saying something positive to me for the first time in more years than I can remember. I noticed Francis smiling as he raised his glass in my direction. Things were going well, I remember thinking to myself. Afterwards, with Cathy's help, I gave our guests their second course – they did not have a choice, but received both my crab cakes and my 'Heart of Texas' smoked barbecued brisket – a somewhat odd combination according to Richard. He redeemed himself with high praise for both food items. Everyone seemed to be enjoying themselves which caused me to be very happy. After everyone had their fill of crab and beef, Cathy brought out trays of her offering, strawberries and ice cream in her hard baked meringue shells. It was all good, bordering on a great meal with everyone feeling relaxed since the wine and cocktails had been flowing abundantly.

Since it was beginning to get a little cool outdoors, I suggested we all move indoors for coffee and a special surprise or two. Ellen had asked me earlier when might be the best time to present Francis with his graduation gift. "In front of all his guests tonight after dinner," was my suggestion. So with some good dark strong coffee in everyone's hand or lap, Ellen asked for our attention.

"Francis, it's time for my gift to you to celebrate your milestone achievement – graduation from the Academy and commissioning into the service of our country." She presented him with a beautifully gift-wrapped box. Excitedly Francis opened it to reveal a beautiful Swiss chronograph watch with a very distinctive 18 carat gold/ sterling silver combination bracelet. Clearly, Francis liked it, and went over to Ellen, picked her off the floor in a bear hug, and kissed her again and again. Ellen was thoroughly enjoying the attention and exclaimed,

"If I had known all it takes was a watch to get that many kisses, I'd have given you one long ago, ha!" We all laughed and were too enjoying the good feelings that were in the air.

Next it was my turn. "Francis, on the day you were born, I purchased a bottle of fine old English Port that was 21 years old with the intention of opening it on your 21st birthday. Tonight I think we are close enough to that day. Here Son is that bottle that I have saved through all the ups and downs, coast to coast moves of a man's life," I said as I produced a small bottle sized crate with straw packing the bottle securely inside. Francis opened it and held up the prized bottle of 1968 Warre Vintage Port. "Son, may we all enjoy a glass of your port?"

"To be sure!" Francis said as he gingerly and slowly opened the old dusty expensive bottle.

"Richard, you being the wine connoisseur of this group, I'd like to ask you to help us all enjoy our first tastes of Francis' vintage port wine." Richard was absolutely delighted to be called on in this capacity.

"As Francis pours everyone a sample, I'd ask you all first to look closely at the wine in the glass." Holding the glass up to the light, Richard said, "First, I think it has a very pleasing appearance, brilliant, but exceptionally deep in color. Next, let's all take in the aroma. Swirl it and breathe deeply the fragrance – it just shimmers with hints of blackberry, spice, and maybe a little cocoa. Now let's take a mouthful onto the tongue. What do you sense? Anyone?"

Lori was the first to speak up, "Dad, it's heavy and dense; there's a surprising texture to it."

"Very good. That is my view also; the viscosity grabbed my attention before anything else. Now, what is next? Is the wine sweet or does it have a crisp acidity with tastes of tannins?"

Francis was next, "Richard, it has both, but in nice balance, I'd say."

"Francis, you nailed it. I think it has an exceptional balance, and the finish is long and strong on the tongue. Do you notice that lovely accent of black pepper perking up the fruit? Francis, it's one of the best ports I have ever experienced."

Everyone cheered. "Is that cheer for the wine or for Richard's incredible critique?" I asked the group.

"It's a fine balance of the two," came from Ellen, sitting at the side of Francis and Lori.

"I'll drink to that," said Cathy. Clearly the evening had taken on a sparkle that probably surprised everyone. After all, there were four divorced adults who had been married to each other in the room, and they all were getting along and having fun together.

Francis put his arm around Lori, and announced, "This is the best, if also the weirdest, party of my life. Thank you every one for being here. I cannot wait to see how the rest of the week goes with a start like tonight."

"You just practice your speech for graduation, young man", came from Ellen, who was standing very close to Richard.

"Yes Ma'am," Francis saluted his mom's direction.

The evening was a hit, but it was winding down. "Richard, why don't you take Ellen back to Eastport in our car? Francis is staying here tonight with his car, so we'll have transportation as needed. Ellen knows how to get back to Eastport, right Ellen?" I suggested. "Tomorrow morning at 1100 hours is the Color Parade, the last parade of Francis' Midshipman career. I suggest we all meet at the south end of Worden Parade Ground near Gate 8 at King George Street and Maryland Avenue around 10:30 in the morning. Richard, you and Ellen as well as all of us will need a photo ID to enter the Yard ever since the 9-11 disaster. Does that sound okay with you, Francis?"

"Perfect! And thanks Richard and Mom and Cathy for being here!"

"Hey, what about me?" from Lori, feeling left out.

"Lori, I have a special 'Thank you' to pass along to you down by the boathouse later." We all whistled together at the same time. It was great to see the younger two getting along far better than any of us could have imagined.

As everyone had left us alone in the kitchen cleaning some of the clutter before bedtime, I pulled Cathy close, kissed her, and asked, "Any residual nervous doubts about the weekend, my Love?"

"Just one. Can you make love to me quietly with the kids in the house downstairs tonight?"

"In a New York minute!" I said laughing.

"No, I want a full hour of your best efforts."

The first day was exactly as I hoped – memorable in the best of ways.

CHAPTER 18

Thursday morning began just as beautifully luminescent on the water as the earlier part of the week. Today the June Week activities for Francis got underway fully with the morning's Color Dress Parade at Worden Field followed by an afternoon garden party at the Superintendent's Quarters. Cathy, Lori, and I got dressed and drove over to the Academy where we would meet Richard and Ellen at the Alumni Hall near Worden Field. It was warm; I had worked up a sweat by the time we caught up with Richard and Ellen. "You ladies look magnificent in your summer dresses," Richard said of all three women. "I haven't seen that dress, Cathy. It's very pretty.

"Bret bought it for me in Ireland last Fall." was Cathy's simple response. Both Richard and Ellen looked at each other. Since I really did not wish to dwell on that topic a moment longer on this particular day, I asked Richard if he and Ellen had a comfortable first night at the Eastport House. Both of them were instantly engaged in telling us how great a place it seemed. "What a find! I cannot imagine a better place from which to explore Annapolis," Richard exclaimed. We had some lemonade to cool ourselves from the walk over across the Yard from where we had parked. After half an hour of visiting, we heard the Navy band start playing in the distance. I suggested we that we should begin our walk over to the reviewing stands if we wanted to get a good seat. As we approached the south end of Worden Field, we noticed it was filling already at 10:30 hours, fully a half hour before the final Dress Parade of the year was to begin. We found some good seats near the midpoint of the stands about ¾ of the way up. It was funny to watch how the group automatically arranged itself as I led everyone to the seats – me, Cathy, Lori, Richard, and then Ellen. I looked around; there were people everywhere as far as the eye could see, even across the river, lining the bridge.

"Bret, does the Parade always bring out so many people?" Cathy asked.

"The weekly parades during nice weather are always popular and well attended by the townspeople and guests, and visiting parents/relatives, but especially so during Commissioning Week for one big reason."

"Why is that?"

"You'll see in a few minutes" And before I had finished talking, we all heard the roar off in the distance of jet aircraft approaching. Here they come....the Navy's Blue Angels flight team. The six F-18 Hornets painted in the distinctive blue and gold colors approached from the north end of the field down the Severn River really low, really loud. They came screaming across the field, and just when they were even with the Sailing Center on the corner of the Yard, they shot straight up. For 15 minutes we were treated to the most amazing flight show.

"What a recruiting tool!" Cathy exclaimed.

The sun was very warm, but not unpleasant as the excitement died a bit from the Blue Angels, and the Color Parade began. The full Brigade of Midshipmen in their dazzling Full Dress White Uniforms began to march onto the field. "Wow, this is impressive," said Lori. Clearly she and the others were enjoying the parade, not something most people would get to see on a normal college graduation weekend.

"Lori, if you think it's hot for us, just imagine yourself down on the parade ground dressed in a high neck wool tunic in the midst of a company of 100 other men, all carrying a heavy rifle and marching in step with each other."

"I'd like that, Bret – in the middle of 100 men? Sounds great!" Lori was laughing and caused us all to smile in agreement.

Soon, Ellen looked our way and pointed, "Lori, there's Francis. Do you see him in the middle of the Brigade staff?

"Wow! He's leading the whole show!"

"Although Francis would normally be marching with his 17th Company, today he was part of the lead group in his role as Spring Semester Brigade Commander, the top ranking Midshipman from a military organization point of view," I explained. "Here at the Academy, we do not have fraternities/sororities, but instead military companies, divided into two regiments of three battalions each. Now when I was here 30 years ago, we had 36 companies; today it's 30. Francis' company is the 17th Company. You can see it on the guidon flag at the head of the unit."

The Navy Band gave way to the Academy's Drum & Bugle Corps. When all the companies of Midshipmen were on the field, Francis saluted with his dress sword to the Admiral and his reviewing staff of the Commandant, a Senator and two Congressmen. I was so very proud of Francis, and noticed his mother Ellen looking my way with a smile on her face. Everyone was happy, but none more than I. All companies passed in review and marched off the parade ground. I gathered our group at the foot of the viewing stands and said, "Follow me; you will want to see the rest of the final first class parade tradition." I led them along Chauvenet Walk toward Michelson Hall and up to Radford Terrace fountain. There all the firsties were engaged in jumping into the fountain's pool in their full dress uniforms. It was all but over, a traditional conclusion like so many classes before of the grueling, but rewarding four years by the Severn. Francis looked out as he was climbing from the pool and saw Lori. He immediately ran over and embraced her in his wet clothes. She squealed like a very young school girl. The two of them were having an obvious good time as we, the parents looked on in happy amusement. We adults adjoined to the Drydock Restaurant over in Dahlgren Hall for some cool drinks while Francis and Lori took some time together to walk out to Triton Point on the seawall. "Well, what did you all think of the Color Parade?" I asked as we all relaxed over our iced drinks.

"It was one of the best, most impressive shows I've ever seen. It really got my patriotic blood flowing," Richard answered.

"How was it for you, Ellen, after seeing several of these events before?" Cathy asked.

"Well, I am speechless. Watching your only offspring lead 3,000 men and women in full dress uniforms right past the reviewing stand of Admirals, Captains, and members of Congress....how could you ever have imagined this day when you were giving birth?" was Ellen's answer that came with some tears.

It was a moment of mixed emotions. We all were thinking of years gone by and experiences that were now long past. "The future of our country is in good hands as these sons and daughters go out to serve, defend, and eventually lead our country," I said. Clearly, I too was showing a vast amount of pride.

By the time Lori and our drenched Francis came back into the restaurant, we all were ready to go and rest before dressing up for the Superintendent's Garden Party at his residence, Buchanan House, which is beside the Chapel. It was decided that Francis would go into Bancroft Hall and get a dry white dress uniform, and then accompany Cathy, Lori, and me back to the cottage while Richard and Ellen would return to Eastport. At 1630 hours we all would meet at the band shell in front of the Chapel, and walk together over to the new Admiral's house and party.

Cathy made us some soup and sandwiches once back at the cottage. We just lazed around outside in the lounge chairs...Lori and Francis made themselves comfortable in a hammock near the waterline. "Look at those two," I said. "I've got some good feelings about them both. They look like they have been dating for months instead of just meeting on Tuesday for the first time."

"Well, Bret, in fairness, they both have been hearing about us for some eight months now, Lori about you from me, and Francis has been hearing about me from you, right? It should make the getting acquainted with a potential step-sibling, a lot easier knowing how much we care for each other. Our kids should be just as neat as we are, don't you think?"

"Of course, you are right, Darling, but we may have something more than just step children on our hands?"

"Bret, if you are thinking what I think you are, then I would just ask to keep it under your cap for now. I would hate to jinx anything that might be developing."

"Gosh, I love you for your cool, calm, collected nature. Did I ever tell you that?"

"Yes, but a girl can't hear it often enough!"

Before we finished our talk, the telephone rang. Cathy got it, and I heard her say, "Sure, come on out. We will be ready before long."

"Who was that on the phone you were telling to come on out? We've got the garden party to attend."

"It was Richard. He and Ellen are dressed and ready to visit some more with us before the evening party."

"My gosh! You were talking to your Ex and you actually asked him over here?" I queried.

"Pretty amazing how forgiving I am, right, Bret?"

"Not much could make me happier than good relations all around. I'm hoping Ellen becomes settled with the idea of me spending the rest of my life with you. Richard seems acquiescent about it all." I walked over and kissed Cathy. "Thanks for being so wonderful about everything."

"Darling, I thought you were nuts – totally bonkers when you first told me about the thoughts you were having at asking Richard to meet Ellen and come here for Francis' graduation."

"And now?" I asked with a smile.

"Well.....I guess I have to admit it has gone well. It probably has been more fun for Ellen because she has someone to be with, and it seems she likes Richard. Who, besides you, Mr. Matchmaker himself, could have foreseen this happening?"

The doorbell rang. "Maybe I should welcome Richard and his 'date', " I said, laughing as I went to the door. As I opened the door for the two of them, I was stunned at how good they both looked. For all his faults, Richard in his silk suit was a good looking man, and the woman on his arm was so beautiful as to not be recognizable to me, but it was Ellen in one of her finest cocktail dresses.

I opened a fresh bottle of sparkling wine and poured everyone a glass. Lori came in from outside and ran over to her dad, hugged him and asked, "Who is this beautiful woman accompanying you?" which made a few immediate points with Ellen.

"Good to see you, Lori. I think you may have to ask Francis about my date. She does look beautiful, doesn't she?" Richard asked.

Ellen put her arms around Lori. "I hope you can be the publicist for my son when he runs for office! You are good with the blarney, ha!"

"Ellen, everyone here makes a good looking couple. It's fun going out with the older generation when they are as classy as you guys."

I laughed so hard, I almost spilled my glass of wine.

"Bret, you don't take that 'older generation' as offensive, do you?" asked Ellen.

"No, I can't object to the truth, I guess."

We enjoyed visiting and laughing until Cathy pointed out the time. "We still need to get prettied up. Ellen, you and Richard make yourselves completely at home while we get dressed." Lori and Francis had begun earlier and were nearly finished when we left to go upstairs. Soon it was time to depart; we were able to get everyone into the rented SUV without getting any of us too wrinkled.

Walking up to the Superintendent's House, Francis asked, "Dad, did you ever do any midnight pep rallies here as a Plebe?"

"Oh, gosh, yes...dead of winter in our bare arms, yelling to "Beat Army" until we could hardly talk. Hard to believe that was 34 years ago!"

We entered the Admiral's quarters and were escorted to the beautiful garden outside where many dignitaries were gathered around the fountain and the bar. They were talking to the new Superintendent, Vice Admiral Mike McNaulty, who was in the Class of '74. He broke away from his other guests and came over to Francis to meet us. "Francis, I've wondered about your family...is this your mother and father?

"Yes Sir, this is my extended family." Introductions to the Admiral and his wife were made.

"And Lori, what do you think of Commissioning Week so far?"

"Admiral, my Grandfather, Captain Schuyler, used to tell me of his Academy days, but, until this week, I had no idea just how very special a place it is. You must be very proud to have been named Superintendent of this historic place."

"Lori, you are very perceptive. I still have not digested the honor given me. Great naval men throughout history have occupied this house. I am all but overwhelmed." Turning to Francis, he said, "Francis, I'd hold on to her if I were you. She will enhance your career."

Francis looked over to Lori, smiled, and said, "Thank you, Admiral. I hope to be able to take your advice!"

The afternoon and evening were delightful on all levels. A combo of Navy musicians was playing up on the terrace. Before the party ended, Lori and Francis were dancing cheek to cheek. The somewhat unusual part was that I and Ellen and Richard and Cathy were also able to enjoy a dance. "Just look at that. Whoever would have thought my Dad and Mom would ever again be dancing together?" Francis whispered in Lori's ear.

"And my Dad and Mom! This is just too incredible. Francis, do you think we might all be able to get along like this in the future?"

"That, my dear lady, might depend on you."

"What do you mean by that statement?"

"If we, you and I, put something together long term, I think it might happen – that we all might be gathering together in the future for holidays and other occasions."

"Put something together for the long term? Why Midshipman Harte, again, whatever do you mean by that?" Lori was showing her excitement.

"Lori, it's just that I have enjoyed the last few days more than any in my life until now, and I would like to have those feelings continue. When you are around me, or I am thinking of getting to be around you, my heart just skips, my feet want to dance. And I like feeling like that!"

"Francis, perhaps we need to talk more about your feelings."

"And yours," Francis whispered with enthusiasm in Lori's ear.

"We might be able to come to some sort of accommodation about your feelings before you are commissioned tomorrow. What are you doing after the Admiral's party?"

"Sitting with you down at the boathouse at the cottage with a bottle of wine and talking about the future. What do you think?"

"I will be there Francis, and in a lot less clothing than I am wearing now!"

The Admiral's garden party ended around 8:00 PM. The six of us decided we were not hungry after all the canapés and hors d'oeuvres we had taken in at the party. "It's too early to call it an evening just yet," I said. "Why don't we all gather back at the cottage and talk about tomorrow and the weekend?" It was agreed, and we all headed out, Lori and Francis with Richard and Ellen in Francis' new car. Cathy and I led the way in the rented SUV.

Once back at the cottage, Lori and Francis both went rushing inside to change. The rest of us settled out back on the deck while I took everyone's drink orders. Richard was a martini drinker, both Cathy and Ellen liked white wine, and I had my usual scotch and soda. The younger members came out attired in swimsuits. "We might go for a kayak ride in the moonlight," Francis said.

"Take a whistle and a strong light in case of a man overboard," I laughed.

"Got it, Dad," replied Francis. And off they went, almost running down the deck in the dark, just the moon lighting their way.

"Oh, to be young again," Ellen said with a sigh. "It's truly remarkable to watch the two of them."

"What do you mean?" I asked.

"Bret, it just surprises me how well the two of them seem to be getting along. I mean, they were strangers until Tuesday – two days ago, and now they seem like they've known each other for years."

"I agree it's a good thing, a very good thing. Look at all of us. Whoever heard of four divorced people sitting together on vacation, each with the other's former spouse in the room? Forgive me, Ellen, but you and Richard also seem to be relating well, right?"

Richard pitched in, "What is not to like about this woman?" as he took her hand in his. Ellen looked at Richard, clearly pleased at all the attention from her 'date'.

"Well, guys, I am prepared to keep the libations flowing to savor this moment in time. Pressing on and thinking I probably was proceeding on very thin ice, I said, "Cathy and I just might have to invite you both to our wedding. The kids will both be there of course."

The porch was silent for a moment as the full weight of that proposal was absorbed by all. Richard was the first to speak, "I'd like to be there if Ellen will come too."

Although it was somewhat dark on the terrace with only a few candle lamps providing light, I could see an absolutely amazed look on Cathy's face. "Did I say something wrong? Is everything okay, Cathy?"

"No, Bret, everything is just fine, really. I'm thinking that if you had made that statement one month ago, I would have thought you were certifiably nuts – just gone over the edge of reality. But tonight, I think I too am ready to ask, 'Would you both come?' "

Not a sound was heard except for the call in the distance of a loon. After an uncomfortable period of silence, Richard was the first to speak, "I guess it all hinges on Ellen."

More silence. Finally, Ellen said, "If you all are waiting on me, then the decision is 'Yes'!"

Cathy got up and went to Ellen and hugged her. Looking at the two of them, I said, "Richard, no hug is required, but I will join you in a martini. Make one of your West Coast specialties for me?"

"Sure thing, Bret," and off to the kitchen we went.

Before Richard had finished stirring together his pitcher of martinis, we head the women shrieking out on the porch where we had just left them. Richard and I ran out to see what all the commotion was about, and we saw both Lori and Francis standing there dripping wet.

"Okay, give a report, Midshipman Harte," I said laughing.

"Well, we decided to go skinny dipping in the moonlight, Dad, but the kayak tipped over before we could get undressed."

"Cathy, he is his Father's son," Ellen said shaking her head.

"Oh, I was hoping he had a bit of you in him, Ellen," Richard was heard to exclaim.

Then Francis spoke up, "It was Lori's idea actually."

Lori turned red and gave Francis a big blast with her fist. We all laughed. I suggested the two of them go and change into some dry clothes, and then join us for a nightcap. When they returned, Francis said, "We have something to discuss with you. Please sit down, all of you."

We all looked at each other and did Francis' bidding. "Look, Lori and I do not like this half brother, step sister sort of situation you have placed on us. All of us looked concerned. "We," Francis continued, "would like something different, something more fun. Depending on a lot of unknown factors, we think we are going to attempt something better and richer, like a long-term romantic involvement." With those words, pandemonium broke out among the older members. I started dancing in a tight circle, an Irish reel with Cathy, while

Ellen and Richard were both yelling and actually kissing one another between outbursts.

The kids were dumbstruck! "I've never seen you this drunk in my life, Dad." Francis pronounced. "Lori, I think it's too late for all of them!"

Without further explanations, I said to the group, "Tomorrow is the big day; Francis is graduating and will be introducing the Governor and the Vice-President of the United States. I suggest we all get a good night's sleep and arrive early at the stadium. We can meet up early and after the ceremonies at the north end of the field under my class of 1980 wall plaque."

As Cathy and I cleaned the cottage once everyone had left, we discussed how great the week had gone so far. What a total surprise it was for Cathy, and even I was happy at how well things seemed to be going. It could have blown up in our face, but we were very happy that everyone was getting along so well.

CHAPTER 19

Another morning dawned beautifully sunny and warm. I took coffee to Cathy out on the verandah, and went down the hall and knocked on Lori's door. "Coffee's ready," I said loudly through the door, and went out to the verandah with Cathy. Lori was moving more quickly than I would have guessed after so late an evening. She joined us on the patio in her nightgown. "I must tell you that I am impressed how good you both look without any makeup or fussing. Today is going to be hot in the stadium, so you both need to wear a cool sun dress."

"When do we need to leave, Bret?" Lori asked.

The stadium is going to be crowded when the commencement starts at 11:00, so I'd say we need to be on our way by 9:30 or so. That's what I've told your dad and Ellen...that we would meet them around 10:00 o'clock at the north end of the field.

I cooked up some of my eggs and Texas hash for a quick breakfast. We loaded into the car and headed in towards the Academy. I had a special Alumni parking pass, so we were able to get into the parking area quickly while many others were locked in the long traffic lines. "Bret, it sure pays to plan ahead," said Lori. She was showing her anticipation and excitement at the thought of watching Francis perform his role during the cere-monies. "Are you excited, Bret?" she asked me.

"Oh, my gosh, yes! Does it show that much, Lori?"

"It's going to be a great day, Mom!"

"And to think how hard I tried to sell you on the idea of coming here, Lori. I must tell you it has been abso-lutely terrific so far having you here. All of us men are more relaxed because you have tried so hard. Richard seems completely comfortable, so am I, and I know Francis is having the time of his life with all the atten-tion he is receiving from you, Ellen, and Cathy."

"Bret, it was meant to be! I wouldn't have missed this week for the world."

"Well," said Cathy, "I can hardly wait to see what else is in store for our future, but I am sure it is going to be fun, right?"

We all laughed goodheartedly in agreement.

Suddenly, Lori exclaimed, "There's Dad and Ellen over across the parking lot. They are heading toward Gate 3. Let's run and catch up!"

I stopped the car, "You can go ahead while we find a place to park." Lori was out and running toward Richard almost before I stopped.

"Bret, I do not think I've ever seen her so happily animated as these last few days. I am so glad you orchestrated everything so well, my Darling," Cathy said as she leaned over and kissed me.

"Now cut that out," I said, "before you cause me to return you to the cottage and miss the entire commencement exercises."

We both laughed. She knew that she wielded a power over me like no one ever has. But she also knew how important this day's activities were to me.

"Bret, we can make love every day for the rest of our lives, but today is the only day you can see your son graduate from the Naval Academy."

"Cathy, only once a day for the rest of our lives?" I said with a smile.

"Okay, okay....so I understated it by a factor of 1000, alright?"

I remember thinking how very much I loved this woman.

By the time we walked up to the gate, Lori had already distributed our tickets and was anxious to get into the stands to see just where we were seated. I hugged Ellen, and suggested that this day had been long in coming. "Yes, Bret," she said, "we did a few things well, and Francis and his education was among the best."

It seemed our visiting had just run its course when the ceremony began with the march on of the graduating first class or seniors. One thousand and sixty-eight of them marched onto the field and took their places in the chairs reserved for the graduating first classmen and women. Lori was the first to see Francis as he walked up onto the stage and took his place in the midst of Admirals, Captains, and government officials along with the Governor of Maryland, and the Vice-President of the United States. Off in the distance I could hear the faint roar of jets. "Get ready," I said, "here comes the Blue Angels. No sooner had I spoken than the flyover of six Navy jets all painted in the colors of blue and gold dominated the sky with their presence and tremendous roar. A great cry went up from the crowd. The Blue Angels were definitely always a crowd pleaser. The Superintendent began his remarks with the various officials on the dais adding their comments. Then it was Francis who came to the podium and proposed a cheer for those whom his class was leaving behind, "Hip, hip, hooray!" Three times Francis led the cheer and then he broke into a singing of the Navy Hymn. Everyone of our little group looked at me; I was struggling to keep from tearing up. I was as proud as I would ever be in my life. Next Francis introduced the Governor of Maryland who in turn introduced the Vice-President. We settled in for a rather boring policy speech from the Vice-President, and then, the time came for the swearing in portion of the Commissioning Ceremony. At the end of the swearing in, the Admiral made his pronouncements and all 1,068 former Midshipmen threw their caps into the air simultaneously. As soon as it had started, it seemed it was finished. I, of course, could have listened and enjoyed another hour of the ceremony because this was the culmination of all I had dreamed for my son.

"Well, Lori, it's time for you and me to get into the act," I said as I handed her a package of new Ensign Officer shoulder boards. "Let's get down onto the field so we can each snap on Francis' new officer insignia. Cathy and Ellen, do you have the cameras ready?"

It was bedlam on the field as families and newly com-missioned young men and women were all searching for their loved ones. We were lucky to have planned to meet Francis at our favorite spot under my Class Memorial Plaque. I saluted my son and hugged him. "It's time we get you some officer insignia on that white uniform," I said to Francis. "Lori, will you assist me and place the shoulder boards on his right side as I take care of this side?" We snapped them in place, I hugged Francis, and then, he turned to Lori, bent over and kissed her as if he had been at sea for two years. She was loving every second of this. Suddenly, Francis saw his mother Ellen standing off to the rear, and ran to her and picked her off the ground. "Mom, this is just the greatest moment in my life. I am so thankful you are right here at my side to celebrate all this with me!" He kissed his mom with all the affection that was appropriate.

"Well, Son, it's your day. What would you like to do?" I asked Francis.

"Dad, I have permission to take one of our Navy Ludders 44 yachts out for the weekend. I would really like to get out of uniform and go for a sailing excursion over to the Eastern Shore and back." Francis looked at the rest of the group and asked, "Everyone ready for a bracing sail across the Chesapeake?"

"You're a real sailor? You can sail a yacht?" Lori asked.

"As captain of the Academy sailing team, I think you will be in good hands – all of you, if Dad will help out manning the sheets."

"I'm in. What about you, Cathy" I asked.

"I'm treating if you can get us to a good restaurant on the water over there," Richard exclaimed.

"Okay, then. Let's everybody meet at the Crown Sailing Center by 06:30 hours tomorrow. Bring some warm clothes; even 'though it feels warm on shore, it'll be cool on the Bay."

"Aye-aye, Sir!" Lori piped up.

"For now, how about some champagne and relaxation back at the cottage?" said our new Ensign.

That idea seemed to appeal to everyone. With the heat and exertion we all had been through, the idea of sitting on the deck watching the shorebirds and drinking lemonade instead of champagne sounded just about perfect.

Lori and Francis went with Richard and Ellen while Cathy and I drove together back to the cottage. Cathy made a huge jug of iced fresh lemonade as I made ready the champagne. Once we all had changed into shorts and Hawaiian shirts, I gathered everyone in the dining room where I had iced the champagne. Popping the cork, I poured each of us a glass of the finest bubbly any of us would ever likely experience again. Richard noticed and made a positive comment about the year and brand of what we were about to partake. Holding aloft my glass, "To my Son as he embarks on his career. May he love the ships on which he serves, may they carry him safely on the seas where he is called!" I said almost choking as I spoke. It was an emotional moment.

"Thank you, Dad. It is a grand occasion made even more special by having you all here. It is a most unusual pairing of families, but it is wonderful nonetheless. I am very lucky."

For the first time since we all arrived in Annapolis, time seemed to slow, and we all were able to just sit and unwind, really for the first time this week - a most pleasant afternoon and evening unfolded.

"With all the crab and seafood we've been taking in, how does just plain hamburgers grilled over charcoal outside sound to everyone?" It was a unanimous and enthusiastic 'Yes!' from everyone. As Richard and I prepared the charcoal, him with a martini, and me with my Glenmorangie and water, I asked, "Richard, did you ever think six months ago that you and I would ever be cooking hamburgers together, especially with each other's former spouses?"

"Never, not in a 1,000 years could I have dreamed this scenario!"

"And are you alright so far with the weekend, Richard?"

"Yes, on every level. May I speak freely, Bret?"

"Of course," I said.

"Bret, I also never thought I would be interested, seriously interested in another relationship so soon after the pain of losing Cathy. I am quite surprised how well Ellen and I seem to be with each other. Does she know all the gory details about Cathy and my divorce?"

"No, not a thing, other than what you may have told her. Cathy told me she also has not spoken to Ellen about any of her past with you, including the reason for the divorce."

"Good, Bret, let's keep it that way. I confess to being in the process of developing strong, warm feelings for Ellen, and she, so far has been responsive. Tomorrow night, if we spend the night across the Bay in some guesthouse or B&B, I may suggest she and I share a room to save on expenses. Do you think that might cause any problems with anyone?"

I laughed. "Richard, Ellen, for all her faults is not a spendthrift. She is as tight as Francis' new Navy combination cap hatband, and likely will go for the idea from what I have been observing between the two of you. I'd say, 'Go for it' if you are really comfortable with the idea."

About that time, the two women along with Lori and Francis came out into the back yard where Richard and I were drinking and chatting. "Here's our contribution of lettuce, tomato, pickles, onion, baked beans and potato salad. What are you guys going to provide?" asked Cathy with a smile.

"Well, as Richard tends the fire, I'll be whipping up my secret hamburger meat mix. Ensign Harte, will you and Lori take charge of the drink refills – champagne, lemonade, and cocktails?"

"When I came out from the kitchen, I saw Cathy with her camera taking a snapshot of Richard at the grill standing near Ellen. "Why don't the two of you turn around for a picture? Alright, that's good, except maybe you could put your arm around Ellen, Richard, couldn't you?" Cathy asked in an almost scolding way.

I can bend her over and French kiss her if I have to, but maybe this will do," Richard said laughing as he put his arm around Ellen's waist. Before Cathy could take the shot, Lori stood up and said, "What's this about French kissing? Can Francis and I be next?" Everyone laughed as Francis came over and did to Lori just what Richard had threatened with Ellen – bending Lori over and planting an almost too passionate kiss on her lips.

"Did you get that, Mom or do we have to do it again?" Francis said.

"Digital shots are cheap, Cathy. Either way, take another please." Turning toward Francis, Lori said, "Come here again, Sailor!" as she curled her finger his way.

By the time I had placed all my special patties on the grill, everyone was in stitches laughing as to how the picture taking was going. "Am I going to have to cut you all off the free booze this early in the evening?' I asked.

"No, no, Commander Harte! We are all up for a little fun before the ship sails on tomorrow's dawn. Come join us!"

I poured another Scotch, held it aloft, and toasted, "To fair winds tomorrow!" as we all six ate and drank the night away

CHAPTER 20

A beautiful morning was breaking on the dock at the Crown Sailing Center at 06:30 hours. Francis must not have drunk too much last night because he had gotten up very early and had already been on the dock making everything ready. He had come back to the cottage to pick up Cathy, me, and Lori. Just as we unloaded, Richard and Ellen arrived sharply at our agreed time of 6:30.

"Wow, Dad, this is a disciplined group – everyone dressed and ready to sail," Francis said where all of us could hear.

"Actually, some of us hardly got undressed. The night went fast!" was the comment from Richard.

"Let's get aboard for our trip," Francis said as he led us down three slips to where "Dauntless" was tied up. Once aboard, Francis gave us all a bow to stern tour. "There are three staterooms, but only one head. I suggest you all pick a cabin, and put your belongings in it. Lori, I have already put our things in the aft stateroom, alright?"

"Aye, aye, Captain" Lori smartly saluted. We men made several more trips to the dock, bringing an armload of groceries each time.

"Who's going to eat all this chow in a day and a half?" Richard asked.

"We brought it for the crabs and the seagulls," Francis laughed offhandedly.

It was time to be off; everyone came topside to watch as Francis and I cast off the lines and hoisted the foresail to get us out into the Severn River and Chesapeake Bay. Our destination, St. Michaels, was southeast of our location and a little over 25 miles as a bird flies. Although the day was beginning to look beautifully clear, warm, and sunny, the wind was coming from the south, which was our intended direction of travel. Francis explained to Lori with Cathy listening that we would have to sail close-hauled into the wind. That meant a zig-zag course or tacking into the breeze to get us down to St. Michaels which is from where the wind was coming. And although we would be doing 10 - 12 knots in the strong wind, it would take us over five hours sailing time to reach St. Michaels because of the back and forth zig-zag course.

Although the space below was quite pleasant, everyone wanted to be topside in the sun, salt spray, and to feel the wind and watch the birds. Right away Lori wanted to take the helm. Francis showed her the course he had set and turned the wheel over to her. She was elated to be sailing for the first time; they both were enjoying themselves. I looked at Cathy and smiled; she, too, was at peace and seemed very contented. For me, I was watching something I never thought I'd see – Ellen actually enjoying herself in the company of a man. She had never trusted men much; not her father, not me, and had dated little since our divorce 18 years ago – and here she was today, sitting very close to Richard in an almost affectionate pose. I was very hurt by the divorce, but had never allowed myself to become embittered with the circumstances or with Ellen's course. Today I could not be happier than to see her seeming to be happy in the company of Richard.

It was a great day for Chesapeake sailing. Francis put everyone through their turn at handling the helm of "Dauntless". She was 44 feet in length with a deep keel which was heeled over hard into the wind and slicing quietly through the water with only the slapping of the waves and calls of the gulls overhead to break the serenity of the day. It was romantic; I saw my son with his arms wrapped around Lori, holding her tight against his chest. It was the best of times, scripted better than any one of us could have imagined just a few weeks ago when we were in Denver for Lori's graduation.

The women, feeling domestic urges, went down into the galley, and returned with trays of fresh fruit and glasses of champagne. We all imbibed freely, and by the time we were approaching the harbor at St. Michaels, I was feeling a sense of release and abandon, in the mood for just about anything anyone might suggest. It was Richard who broke my reverie by saying, "I think it's time for me to buy us all a waterside lunch!" We tied up in a slip at the public dock area, and strolled along the boardwalk to a rather elegant, white tablecloth dining establishment, yet one with an open, relaxing look.

Richard interceded for us with the maître'd to get the perfect corner table at the front of the restaurant facing the harbor. Cathy remarked as we were seated how lovely the town appeared, even with the influx of summer tourists. St. Michaels had only 1,500 full time residents, but swelled to several times that with the season. While we were all looking at menus, Richard ordered a couple of bottles of wine to get us started. Richard was turning out to be more than I had ever imagined he would be, given my first meeting with him and the circumstances surrounding that chance meeting – Ireland and the events of last fall seemed so very long ago this afternoon.

"What do you recommend for us, Bret?" Richard asked.

"The crab, oysters, and mussels, and the local striped bass would all be good. If you want something a little different, you might try the bluefish – it has a strong flavor and is very rich and fatty," I answered.

"Rich and fatty does not sound that appealing; I think I'll opt for the striped bass, Bret." The waiter returned with our wine and was helpful in taking our late lunch orders. In a moment of silence after the waiter had left, Lori, held up her wine glass and said, "I'd like to propose a toast. Today I consider everyone of us family, and I would like to celebrate the three events that made this extended family circumstance possible– to Mom for finding Bret in Ireland, to Bret for reaching out to Dad and Ellen, and to Francis for his Commissioning Week that brought us together."

"Yes, Lori...an excellent toast!" I said in joining her and the others with a raised glass. When we finished drinking, and Richard had refilled our glasses, Cathy asked, "Francis, what happens next for you in your Navy job?"

"Well, Cathy, I will be heading for Nuclear Power School near Charleston in late July, so I should be able to see Mom rather regularly during my classes there. In the immediate future, I have to get my things moved down to Mom's house in Charleston, and maybe after that I could squeeze in a trip out to San Francisco."

Lori interjected, "I have not yet even unpacked from my move back home at Dad's; I'll probably make Francis help me in that ordeal and figure out some way to repay him, ha!"

"You mean I am not coming out to experience the romance of San Francisco, but to work?" Francis queried.

"I'm thinking we can probably get both worked in together, Francis," Lori said.

"Well. That is a pleasant surprise," remarked Cathy.

"And what about you and Bret?" Ellen asked Cathy.

"Ellen, I have a new job to prepare for this fall as well as getting my move from the Bay area accomplished. Bret and I want to get married and go away for a couple of weeks in early September before I must hit the ground running as the new editor and publisher of 'Senior Living and Travel' in October."

"Have you set the wedding date and place yet, Cathy?"

"Yes, the date will be around Labor Day, but we still have not decided on a location or planned the guest list, and we are running out of time, Ellen, so the first thing we will probably do back in Dallas is to sit down and nail down the details. Now what are you going to do this summer?"

"Cathy, I have asked Richard to come to Charleston, so I will have the chance to make him some home cooked meals and show him the last vestiges of the old South. I think he will like it all."

"That's wonderful news, Ellen. Richard has been working too hard his entire life. Taking some time off in Charleston is probably better than anything his physician could have ordered. And Francis, what about tonight? Are we staying overnight here in St. Michaels or sailing back to Annapolis?"

"Why don't we all stay the night here?" Lori asked. "Francis, will that work with the sailboat – do we have to have it back in Annapolis tonight?"

"Nope! We're good if a stay over is everybody's wish. We can sail over to The Inn at Perry Cabin – that's a terrific place to stay if they have space. Want to give them a call?

"Okay, how any rooms do we need?" was Cathy's response.

"Lori and I can sleep aboard. Is that alright with you, Lori?" asked Francis.

"Sure, Francis." It was evident that Lori was happy to be asked. Looking at the rest of the group, Richard said to Francis, "If Ellen is okay with sharing a room, then we can get a total of two rooms for the old folks, ha!"

"Okay, but if Richard snores too loudly, I'll be coming down to the dock to sleep aboard the 'Dauntless', " Ellen said laughingly.

We called the Inn. "We're in luck, they've had a couple of cancellations and we can have the rooms. Let's cast off," I said with enthusiasm. Richard paid the check and we all walked hand in hand back to the "Dauntless."

CHAPTER 21

After a leisurely breakfast in the main dining room at the Inn, everyone boarded "Dauntless" and we made ready for the return to Annapolis. It has been the best of times. Everyone was getting along so very well that Cathy had even remarked how surprised she was with the entire weekend. As Francis and I guided the sailboat out into the Chesapeake, everyone was kicked back and enjoying another beautiful summer day in the Bay area. Francis and Lori took over piloting the vessel while Cathy and I relaxed on the bow and Richard and Ellen leaned against the mast taking in the sea spray and watching the gulls that were following us. Lori with her beautiful tan had decided to go forward to ask something of her mom. As she was walking barefoot, Lori caught her foot on the edge of a small deck plate that was sticking up; immediately she shrieked in pain and the blood started running.....too freely. Francis yelled for me to take the helm as he ran to Lori's aid. He calmly asked Lori to sit down on the deck, looked at the wound, and then wrapped a towel tightly around Lori's torn left foot. He scooped her up in his arms and carried her back to the doorway into the galley and berths below. I knew Lori was in good hands because of Francis' first aid skills, and because of the fact that he already cared for Lori more than any of us knew. He dressed the wounded foot and suggested to Lori that she was going to need a few stitches to close the wound once we got back to Annapolis. Francis got the bleeding stopped and gave Lori a shot of brandy to relax her. Then he leaned over to kiss her and said, "Sweetheart, everything is going to be fine, I promise. I am so sorry that deck plate was not properly fastened; I'll see to it that no one else gets hurt like you." Francis carried Lori back outside and placed her gently on top of the cabin where the sun and breeze could be readily felt on her skin.

"Dad, I suggest we set as direct a course as we can to Annapolis; I want to get Lori to the hospital emergency room to have a doctor put a few stitches in her foot to speed healing." Lori said to everyone, "The weekend has been so fine; please do not let my mishap put a pall on any of it — Francis said I am going to be alright."

"Well okay then," Richard said as he put his hand on Francis' shoulder. "You are going to get to carry Lori's bags....all of them... tomorrow as we head to the airport."

There was still plenty of sunlight left when we arrived back at the mouth of the Severn River and the Academy. Francis and I tied up at the Sailing Center dock and got everyone and their gear offloaded. "Dad and Richard",

Francis said, "I am going to take Lori over to Hospital Point and get her foot looked at. I think she's going to need a few stitches. We'll see you all back at the cabin in a couple of hours or less, I hope."

As Francis was driving Lori to the Naval hospital, he said, "Lori, you did not need to tear up your foot to get me alone with you."

"I didn't?" Lori almost seemed disappointed. "Francis, I do want to talk to you, actually invite you to San Francisco for a few days together. Have you spent any time there?"

"Not what I would call quality time. Just a few days here and there between summer cruise assignments, mostly drinking with the guys."

"And chasing girls, right?"

"Well, Lori, we Navy men do have a reputation to uphold, but the stories are much inflated when compared to the real events. If you are serious, then the answer is 'yes!'. I'd love to have you show me around. But before we make any definite plans, let's get your foot doctored, alright?"

Francis was right. The young doctor on duty tonight put five stitches into Lori's foot wound after a thorough cleaning and giving her a tetanus shot. Since her shoe would not fit over the bandages, he gave her an open toed prosthetic device to wear for a couple of weeks.

"Lori, I want to dance with you when I get to the Bay Area, so you will need to follow all the rules to speed your foot's healing, okay?"

"Anything you say, Francis," Lori said with a mischievous smile on her face.

"You keep talking like that and we are going to get along just great," Francis laughed.

As they were driving back to the cabin from the hospital, Lori asked Francis to pull into a park area. She leaned over and kissed him and said, "Francis, this has been the best weekend I have ever experienced. Even with my foot injury, I feel like I have been cared for as no one ever before has, except for Richard. I want to thank you and Bret for everything, I mean inviting me and Dad, something I never thought would happen. It's seems kind of a small miracle to me seeing everyone getting along so well together in what you would think would be a potentially disastrous weekend. I care for you and your family a lot, Francis."

Francis was silent. "Oh dear, did I say something wrong?" Lori asked.

"Lori, I am filled with so many thoughts right now.... hopes, dreams, emotions that I am not sure where to start any conversation. I do know that I would not like to look into my future and not see you there with me. I think we may have started something this weekend that could become the basis for a long-term, sweet and fulfilling relationship. It's crazy to think how much I care for you based on just a few short days together, but I'm sure enough to desire with all my heart to spend more time with you and attempt to grow what we've started. What do you think?"

"I am not sure what love is, but I hope it is very much like what I am feeling right now." Would you take me back to the cabin and down to the boathouse, and make love to me tonight?"

"You're high from the painkillers the doctor gave you, Lori!" Francis exclaimed.

"Maybe so, but I still need you, your body, and your lips on me. Can you do that?"

"My darling, I can do that for the rest of your life if you let me!"

"Is that a proposal? Ensign Harte?"

"Actually, let's save the question until San Francisco, okay? But Lori, I think I have fallen irretrievably in love with you."

"And I, you. Can you speed up? I want you to make love to me in the boathouse now!"

Everyone assembled for breakfast at the cottage on the final day in Annapolis. "You guys came in late last night," was Cathy's first comment directed to Lori and Francis. "And how is the foot?"

"It hurts, but Francis and the Navy doctor both took great care of me and the wound. I'll be back to normal by July 4th, I promise." Lori replied. "And yes, we did come in late; it was my last night to see my naval officer friend, and we had a good time of it!"

What's everybody doing for the Fourth of July?" Bret asked.

"Dad, since you asked, Lori has invited me to San Francisco for a week over the holiday weekend. I haven't really seen the city, and Lori has promised me a tour to equal the one we gave her and Cathy of Annapolis last week. I do not know if Richard has cleared me to stay there at his house or not. Would that be okay Richard?"

"Sure, Francis. We'll make a great time of it since your mother is coming out during the same time frame; I just asked her last night and she said okay."

"Wow! That's great, Mom. With you in Charleston, Lori and Richard in San Francisco, and Dad and Cathy in Dallas, I may never have to get a motel room again for my U.S. travels."

"What about you and Cathy, Bret?" Richard asked. "What are you doing for the holiday? You might as well come out too, and we'll have our second big weekend together of the summer!"

"Cathy? What say you? You have some packing to do over in Tiburon, right?"

Cathy and I had talked about going out to San Francisco to pack up the majority of her furnishings and clothes, but had not actually set a time and date for the transition. We both desired to keep her townhome in Tiburon as an investment property and to have a place to stay when we travelled out West.

"Why not?" Cathy replied. "I guess we all will be seeing each other again soon."

After breakfast amidst a lot of laughter and conversation, everyone began loading into the two vehicles for the trip to Friendship Airport for their individual returns home. Only Francis was not flying; he had to drive to Charleston and stay with Ellen until his Nuclear Power School startup later in the summer.

CHAPTER 22

The month of June fairly evaporated. Cathy's start date at *Senior Living & Travel* was June 15th, and she hit the ground running....hard! She had interviews to conduct, staff to hire, and a management team to build from the ground up. Numerous contacts from a career in publishing were becoming increasingly helpful in her efforts. We still had several days of packing in the Bay Area to get her things brought to Dallas and settled in my house. As a result of the last day conversations in Annapolis, we decided to save the final few days of packing and moving until the weekend of the Independence Day holiday. We would be able to see everyone and finalize our wedding plans in the company of the folks who mattered most, Francis and Lori, and, strange as it might seem....our ex-spouses.

Cathy loved entertaining, but had experienced little in the way of opportunity to do so in her new home in Tiburon, north of the city across the Golden Gate Bridge. She had coordinated with all the family members for an invitation to dinner at her house on Friday night, the 2nd of July. It was at that venue that she and I would announce our wedding plans, date and location, and extend our invitations to family first.

We arrived Thursday morning in San Francisco and proceeded to her place in Tiburon to begin preparations for the Friday night dinner. Lori was at loose ends, just enjoying her summer off without a job yet. She had spent the week showing Francis the romance of San Francisco and environs. When Cathy called to say we had landed, Lori was thrilled and suggested she and Francis come up to visit and to help prepare for Friday evening. They arrived almost before we did. Truly it was good to see the kids and to see that they seemed to be having a deliriously great time together. Francis suggested that he and I go have lunch together so Lori and Cathy could also have some time alone together.

Francis and I drove down to the waterfront for lunch at the grill right on the water. The day and the temperature was just about perfect, sunny and a cool 68E with no wind. We ate outdoors overlooking the city of San Francisco across the bay.

"Well, Son, tell me what is going through your mind Navy-wise and on the romance scene."

"Dad, of course I am excited about Nuclear Power School and beginning my career as a Naval Officer, but the most prodigious situation facing me is what to do about Lori."

"Uh-oh! Is there a problem, Francis?"

"Only that I can't see my future life being successful without her. Dad, she is incredible in every way"

"Perhaps now you can know why Cathy has such a hold on my affections."

"Dad, if Cathy is half so sexy and fun to be with as Lori, then yes, I do know exactly what you are feeling."

"Francis, does Lori know of your feelings?"

"Yes, I believe it is mutual...I mean I think she is expecting me to pop the question anytime."

"And where are you and your mind on that issue. Francis?"

"Dad, I asked Richard what he thought on Wednesday night when we had dinner at his club while Lori was at a bridal shower for one of her Denver class-mates. I asked him if he would grant me the honor of his permission to ask Lori to marry. D'know what he said, Dad?"

"What?"

"He hugged me and said I was the son he never had, and to please do it! Cool, huh? Dad, there would be nothing wrong about me marrying my step-mother's daughter, would there?

"No, certainly not. There are no blood ties between you and Lori – it's just a rather curious situation, but perfectly acceptable, I think."

"So when will you tie the knot, presuming she says yes?"

"There's so much going on right now. I mean, our plans depend on you and Cathy's plans, Dad. We want everything to be a family affair, so when we marry depends on when you and Cathy set a date."

"Family affair! A curious choice of words, Francis. It does seem pretty curious how everything is working out. Francis, Cathy and I are planning a wedding around Labor Day. We certainly want you, Lori, and Ellen and Lori's Dad all there, so it truly will be a family affair."

"Dad, tomorrow evening's dinner will a pretty special event," Francis said with a wink.

"Shall I tell Cathy?"

"No, let it all unfold naturally, and watch everyone's face. It will be an evening to remember!"

"Okay then. I guess I'd better get a bottle or two of Cristal Champagne in case there is something to celebrate."

"Dad, I appreciate your support. Do you suppose Mom will be okay with all this?"

"Francis, she'll be just as happy as I am, because she can see the happiness in you – you're fairly transparent just now, and it's very becoming. It amazes me after all these years that she and Richard seem to be getting on so well together."

"Yes, Dad, they too are becoming quite a couple. Who knows what may happen on that front. You know how cautious Mom has always been. The last few days, she seems like a giddy school girl when she's around Richard."

"Good! That's really good news. I love your mom in my own special way and want to see her experience happiness and fulfillment in the final half of her life. Happiness that goes beyond watching as you and Lori begin a life of your own. She deserves a loving partner; she could do a lot worse than Richard, and Richard can use the discipline that Ellen would bring to his life. Are you ready to go back to Cathy's and see what the girls have cooked up for a menu for tomorrow night?"

"Sure, Dad. Let me pay for your lunch."

"Francis, forget that idea. You need to be saving for a nest egg for all the things you and Lori will be facing in the next few months. I'll pay the check and then race you Ensign Harte around the circle to the car."

"You're on, old man!"

By the time we got back to Cathy's house, the girls had returned and were making lists of all the things they wanted to do for the gala tomorrow evening. "Hi guys," was Cathy's response when she saw us. What do you think about gazpacho and my grilled flank steak with some mashed potatoes with parsnips, green bean casserole, and fresh strawberries and shortcake for dessert?"

"That covers all my favorites," I said.

Francis piped up, "Me, too....lots of strawberries 'though."

"You guys are in charge of the wine" was Lori's comment.

"And what liquor do you need, Cathy?" I asked.

"Anything you desire is probably already in my cabinet...lots of Glenmorangie to be sure!"

"Do you have Dubonnet and Pernod? I remember that Ellen likes both of those aperitifs."

"Well maybe you need to make a run to the store.... those I do not have," replied Cathy.

We had fun visiting for the next hour and decided to go over to Sausalito for an Italian dinner with the kids. Afterwards they both left for Richard's house and to see if Ellen had made it in from Charleston yet.

Friday, the 2nd dawned as beautiful a day as we could possibly have asked for. Based on the cool, sunny, and still forecast, Cathy decided to have our dinner outside on the deck. Francis called mid day to ask if Cathy had a screen for an AV presentation he wanted to show. Although Cathy did not have one, her neighbor did, and she told Francis that she would borrow it and have it ready for him once he, Lori, Richard, and Ellen arrived. We spent the day lazily relaxing, loving, and making a few packing decisions for things Cathy would need back in Dallas this fall. I helped with the meal preparations, so that by 4:00 pm everything was ready to go once the others arrived – they were expected around 6:30.

At 6:30 sharp, the doorbell rang. It was Richard and Ellen and the kids. Cathy grabbed Ellen in her arms and hugged her like a long lost sister she hadn't seen for years. I liked that a lot; that she and Ellen were friends, despite the unusual circumstances surrounding their friendship – it was amazing when you think about it. Richard looked a tad uncomfortable as he entered Cathy's home, the first time he had seen the life she had begun without him. Cathy put her arm around Richard and said, "Come on in and relax, Richard. We all are going to have a great evening."

"Promise?" Richard laughed nervously.

I, too, was impressed how gracious Cathy seemed in light of Richard's unfaithfulness not that long ago. But Cathy seemed very happy and had apparently put all that behind her. Her former spouse of over 30 years was going to eat dinner at her house tonight and she was determined the evening would be devoid of any angst.

"You men can go to the den and get everyone their preferred libation mixed and served. We girls are going to lay out the meal preparations for later."

During cocktails, Francis brought out his PowerPoint presentation from June Week in Annapolis. It was the first time any of us had seen a lot of the photographs from the cottage and the activities we all experienced together back in June. Everyone thoroughly enjoyed Francis's rather creative slide show. It's funny how all of us had changed in only the nearly three weeks since we all first met. We all seemed like good friends, if not outright family in that short span of time.

After viewing and laughing throughout the show, I asked for everyone's attention. "Cathy and I have decided to go forward with our wedding a bit sooner than we earlier had anticipated because of her new job and attendant work schedule. It's going to be Saturday of the Labor Day weekend."

"This September.....that's scarcely two months from now?" Ellen asked as she looked over at Richard.

"And where, Mom?" asked Lori.

"Yes, in answer to Ellen's question," I responded. "And as to the location, we have all just been looking at our site.....Annapolis." The room got quiet for a moment as the other four were thinking about what I had just said.

"What church, Mom? Or is it going to be in the Academy Chapel?" was Lori's next question.

Cathy spoke up and I sat down. "Of course it's short notice, but we want you all there. Unfortunately, right after we finished our time at the cottage, the owner, Admiral Westin, who owned the property, passed away from a heart attack. Because his wife had been gone for some time before, and because of money issues, Admiral Westin's adult children wanted to dispose of the cottage. When we were settling our rental amount with Nick, the Admiral's oldest son, he asked us if we might know of anyone who would be interested in the cottage. Bret and I were surprised to say the least, but said we might be interested. Bret threw out a ridiculously low immediate cash offer and Nick was not offended. He said that he would speak to his sister about our offer. The fantastic news is that we are now the owners of the property; we signed the papers last week. Bret and I and, I assume, you all too so enjoyed our special time together there, that we have decided the backyard facing the Chesapeake is where Bret and I will exchange our vows. Now for comments....what say you four? Can you make that date in Annapolis?"

It was quiet. Finally Francis asked if he could have our undivided attention. "Mom, Dad, Cathy, and Richard, when I first saw Lori at the baggage claim in the BWI terminal back just days before graduation, I suspected, even hoped, that some sort of really good step-sibling bond might develop between us. Well, it did and a lot more. I love her, and I can tell you it's not like a brother for his sister...it's like your love for Cathy, Dad...over-the-top and forever." At that moment, Francis walked over to Lori, knelt in front of her, opened a box with a stunning diamond ring inside it, and said to Lori, "Lori, my darling, I cannot imagine my life without you in it, just a touch away from my heart and my every breath. Will you do me the magnificent honor of becoming a Mrs. Harte like your mother?"

There was an uncomfortable silence....prolonged silence. Suddenly Lori began sobbing uncontrollably, threw her body at Francis, and said, "I thought you were NEVER going to ask! Yes, a thousand times yes, is my answer!"

Francis turned toward me and toward Cathy, and made the following remarks, " Dad and Cathy, the timing of our decision is a bit difficult, what with my Nuclear Power School start date and Lori's desire to go on to graduate school somewhere, on top of your wedding in Annapolis. I have a question for you....would your min-ister give us a discount for doing two weddings at the same time in the cottage backyard?"

I laughed, but Cathy shrieked. There was all kinds of chatter going on between every member in the dinner party. "Let's all have another drink, and then talk about all these new developments." Richard and I went over to the bar and began making all new drinks around. When everyone had taken a sip of their second drink, Richard said, "Well, guys it's my turn to have a say. First I am so totally in favor of Francis becoming my son-in-law. He's like the son Cathy and I never had. The only thing better would to always be around whenever he visited his mom. To clear up any confusion you might be having, Bret, that pastor you have picked....would he do a three way ceremony?" At that moment, pandemonium reigned. Everyone was laughing, the women crying, and Richard drinking his martini all the way. It was a full ten minutes before any kind of order was restored.

"Richard, have you talked to Ellen about this?" Cathy asked. Ellen spoke up and said, "Richard asked me to marry him two nights ago. Cathy, you are going to be my in-law in more ways than one....more like a sister really, and boy, o'boy can we ever have some interesting discussions about the men in our lives."

"Now that will be off limits, Ellen," I said with a smile on my face.

"As the oldest person in the room, I say 'Hell, let's do it', " was my initial response.

"How on God's earth are we going to pull this off with so little time," Lori asked.

"If everyone is on board with the idea, then we need to start the planning tonight after dinner."

"I'm for it" came from Francis.

"We're in," was the answer from Richard for both him and Ellen.

"Oh, Dad, this is going to be a blast...an absolute blast!" was Lori's comment. Next thing I knew, everyone was hugging everyone, causing me to spill what was left of my Scotch all over Cathy's new sofa. While Cathy was dabbing up the spilled drink, I went over to the bar refrigerator and took out a clear bottle of Louis Roederer Cristal Champagne, popped the cork, and poured everyone a glass. "A toast to the new young couple on their first marriage, and to the rest of us on our second!" I said lifting my glass high.

Needless to say, conversation over diner outside on the back deck was lively as wine flowed and Cathy's marinated flank steak dinner was devoured totally.

"The next 24 - 48 hours will be critical in getting a handle on the guest list, invitations, wedding attire, bridesmaids, groomsmen, caterer, photographer, flowers, travel, honeymoons, etc., etc." I said as we ate dessert and drank more of the second bottle of Cristal.

"I think everyone needs to stay here tonight," Cathy said. "I mean we are all so lubricated, there's no way I want any of my new family driving away tonight. Tomorrow, we can all go down to the Swedish Bakery on the water for breakfast and a planning session overlooking the San Francisco skyline."

"I'm sold," from Richard.

"Us too," from his daughter.

"Now, I don't want to hear of any backouts at breakfast, after we all have slept on this wild plan. It will be history making," I said.

"It might even make the pages of *Senior Living & Travel* if I do say so as the Editor-in-Chief," came from Cathy smiling.

CHAPTER 23

The Weddings

July and August simply evaporated quicker than anyone of us could have imagined back in San Francisco on the Independence Day weekend when the initial plan was formed for this unusual day that was about to begin. With a great measure of good luck, it seemed everything had come together without a single catastrophe. Dashed hopes, plans, and setbacks often happen when planning one wedding, but three at the same time....? I am the eternal optimist, but even my best expectations were met, maybe even exceeded so far, with everything coming together better than any of us could have hoped. The weather looked to be nearly perfect by our 4:00 PM starting time. Since Navy's opening football game was away, there were adequate hotel and B&B rooms available for our nearly 400 invited guests, almost all of whom were from out of town.

The cottage with a fresh coat of paint and special plantings that Cathy had arranged never looked better. By the time all 400 plus white lawn chairs had been set up in the backyard of the cottage, it had been a fight to get a small dance floor, two bars and a buffet line squeezed in along with a few tables for eating after the ceremony, but it seemed like it might work fine. I had once complained about how much grass there was to mow because of the size of the pie-shaped lot, but today we needed every bit of it.

The women involved all stayed together at the cottage while Francis, Richard and I bunked at the same B&B in Eastport where Richard and Ellen had stayed for the June Week festivities when Francis was commissioned. The people we all wanted in the wedding party for the most part were available and excited to be participating in so unusual an affair. The minister who was to perform the service was an old friend and retired Navy Chaplin, Commander Wayne Fox from my class at the Academy. Richard's best man was an attorney friend from Washington, D.C., Jack Montgomery. Francis chose his Academy roommate, Roy Mast, to stand beside him, and I enlisted my physician in Dallas, Captain Harold Whitson, USN Retired, to be my best man. I had been there for him in his first wedding years ago, a wedding that unfortunately had not worked out.

One of the big decisions was who was going to walk the ladies down the aisle, since both Ellen and Cathy's fathers had passed on. Of course Richard would be giving away his daughter, Lori. And although it was way beyond what would be considered normal, we all jointly decided that I would walk Ellen down the aisle and that Richard would be doing the same for Cathy. I am not sure if that has ever happened before in normal

American weddings, but that became the consensus of our family group. Yes, weird, but it became the plan.

Far more than we expected actually called and emailed to say they were coming. It seemed as if all our friends wanted to be a part of so unusual a weekend. The champagne bill was going to be double what I had first anticipated, ha!

We rang a ship's bell at 1600 hours sharp. The guests all took their seats as our spectacular sound system that Francis' friends had installed began playing the traditional Mendelssohn Wedding March. The colors the ladies had picked were a pale yellow for the mothers and traditional white for the new first time bride. Richard first walked Cathy down the aisle and left her beside me. I then left to go to the back of the audience and walk Ellen down the aisle to stand beside Richard. Finally, Richard left and brought his stunningly beautiful daughter Lori down to stand beside Francis. I have to admit that all three of the women were knock dead gorgeous in appearance. The all day of beauty at the expensive salon had done its magic. After the audience had settled from all the whispers and comments, Chaplin Fox looked out over the group and said, "I have been an ordained minister for over 30 years, but I must tell you I have never presided over so unusual a ceremony....not one wedding, not two, but three all taking place at the same time and place. And never have I married a young bride and her father and her mother and her fiancé's mother and father all on the same day. Now I am going to ask everyone's indulgence as I help identify for you all the players in this most unusual day's ceremony. First we have Ensign Francis Harte here to marry Lori Lewis. Please raise your hands for our guests. Fine. Now will the parents of the bride please raise your hands?" Cathy standing beside me and Richard standing beside Ellen both raised their hands. "Next will the parents of the groom please raise your hands?" At that moment, Ellen and I both raised our hands. "So you see, the Father of the bride will marry the Mother of the groom today, and the Father of the groom will soon be the husband of the mother of the bride. Has everyone got that? Now let us begin..... We are gathered today to join these couples in holy matrimony........"

Chaplin Fox completed a marvelous, if complicated, ceremony without any hesitation or mistakes? When he stated that the husbands could now kiss the brides, everyone on the long platform kissed everyone. I kissed Cathy, of course, and then Ellen and Lori. Richard responded by doing the same in reverse. The audience all stood and clapped as we six slowly walked down the aisle to some rather rousing music from ABBA inserted into the program by Francis' Academy friends.

We all had thought the party after the ceremony might go on until 10:00 or 11:00 p.m., but the last of the guests did not leave until after 2:00 a.m. The food, Maryland crab cakes, fresh chowder, and Texas barbecue, coupled with a great open bar and good music and dancing caused everyone to tell us they had never been to a better wedding and reception. We, every one of us, was immensely happy, but also exhausted as we went in different directions – Richard and Ellen to the B&B in Eastport, Francis and Lori to an old historic downtown

hotel, as Cathy and I stayed at the cottage to super-
vise the cleaning of the yard and house for which we
had paid extra to the caterers to do it no matter how
late in the day. Sunday afternoon we all were going to
BWI Airport to begin our separate honeymoon vaca-
tions. Richard had decided to honor Ellen's long held
wish to go to North Africa to Tangier, Casablanca and
Marrakech. The kids wanted to do London and Paris,
and of course, Cathy and I both wanted to go back to
where it all had started — The Craggy Rock Lodge
in Ireland. As it worked out, all our joint itineraries
passed through London's Heathrow Airport, so we all
were flying together out of Baltimore, at least as far as
London, late on Sunday afternoon.

CHAPTER 24

Craggy Rock Lodge

Driving down the tree shaded lane toward the Craggy Rock Lodge, Cathy leaned over and kissed me and said, " How different, almost unbelievably so, are the feelings I'm having today compared to just a year ago when I was being dropped off by a cab at the Lodge. Can you believe all that has happened in just 12 months?"

"No, my Darling, it has not yet sunk in. My son, whom I love, has graduated from Navy and married the second most beautiful woman in the world. My ex is married and happy, and I do not have to have dinner alone ever again in the Lodge's dining room. Extraordinary!"

When we drove up to the front of the Lodge, Mick saw us coming and went running inside. By the time we stopped near the front door, everyone, literally everyone who worked for Cathleen and Reginald were waiting for us to get out of the car. It was like a homecoming as all the staff hugged us and smiled beamingly. Mick said,

"We just knew it would work out when you left under difficult circumstances last year. You looked so good as a couple, it just had to happen. So you're now all legal with a church wedding and everything, right?"

"Mick, I've got photos for you all to see, but first, I need a drink."

"Yes, Mr. Harte! Wait until you see my wedding present." With that he produced a 25 year old oversized bottle of Glenmorangie Scotch, and asked if he could open it for all us to toast the new bride.

"Right now, Mick!"

After we all had finished the drinking of the toast, Mrs. O'Doyle stepped forward, "Mr. And Mrs. Harte, Reggie and I along with all our staff would like to invite you to our own reception for both of you this evening at 6:00 PM in the bar. Will that conflict with any plans you've already made?"

"How very thoughtful, Cathleen," was Cathy's enthusiastic response. Looking to me, Cathy asked, "Would that be okay with you, Honey?"

To both women I said, "I'm thinking that would be a perfect start to our honeymoon. Yes, thank you," as I squeezed Cathy's hand.

When we came downstairs and went into the bar for what I thought would be a somewhat impromptu party, both of us were all but overwhelmed. Surprisingly elaborate were the decorations, food, and music the Lodge and staff had prepared for us. For the next hour Cathy and I euphorically ate, drank, and exchanged hugs with everyone from the scullery maids to Reginald and Cathleen themselves. Finally, Reggie (Mr. Exhall) held his champagne glass high and struck it several times with a spoon to get every-one's attention.

"Bret and Cathy, the employees at Craggy Rock Lodge have a very Irish wedding gift for you both as you begin your married life together." With that he produced a small, shoebox sized present, and gave it to me.

"May we open it here?" I asked as I handed the exqui-sitely wrapped box to Cathy.

"Yes, of course," from Mrs. Exhall.

Cathy was as excited as a young first time bride as she eagerly, but carefully opened the gift. Peeling away a surprising amount of protective wrapping, Cathy gasped as her efforts revealed a stunning 8" Tyrone Crystal Bronaugh Wedding Bell. Engraved on the bell was:

Bret & Cathy
September 4, 2010

With the crystal bell was a frame worthy engraved card which Cathy gave me to read aloud...

Legend of the "Make-Up" Bell
*For centuries in Ireland, the tradition has been
to give engaged or newlywed couples a crystal
"Make-Up" Bell. This bell is to be given a place
of honor in their home. It is to be rung when one
partner is ready to "make-up" and end any quarrel
that may take place during their marriage. It is
expected that each partner take turns ringing the
bell, and not the same partner every time.........*

When I finished reading the card aloud to everyone, Cathy began to cry. Concerned, I took her hand with a puzzled look on my face.

"Cathleen, Reggie, and all of you here – this is the most beautiful and meaningful gift we have received as a result of our nuptials. It WILL occupy a prominent and visible place in our home in Texas. I hope we never use it, but the chances are that Bret will have to ring it someday, ha! You all are the best acquaintances anyone could have. Bret and I would very much enjoy building a longterm friendship with every one of you into the future. Thank you....thank you!"

Our honeymoon was beginning. Cathy and I would recreate every activity of a year ago; it would be even more fresh and intense than it was then, so much was my love for her.

May you all find such a love!

ABOUT THE AUTHOR

After college at the Naval Academy and the University of Texas and a brief stint in the military, Leland began his career in publishing with The New York Times and Better Homes & Gardens. An equal amount of time was spent in design and construction headquartered out of Dallas, Texas.

The initial seeds of this first novel germinated in 1992 on a trip to the Republic of Ireland, a country where a person can easily step back to a time and place of beauty, romance, honesty, and friendliness that has all but disappeared in our fast paced world today.

Today Leland, unmarried, lives with his miniature schnauzer, Gracie, in the Dallas area. In his limited free time, he travels between the Pacific Northwest, the Door Peninsula of Wisconsin, and attempts to catch a few shows and Christmas shop annually in the British Isles.

A LAST WORD FROM THE AUTHOR

One of the joys of being a writer is getting together with other book lovers in readers' groups, book clubs, and libraries. My attendance in any of those venues usually results in new friends and knowledge, and I often learn more than I impart.

If you like books, ideas, and travel, I would enjoy meeting you/your friends. Getting together is easier than you may be thinking. Here are some ideas....

In Person If your group is in the Dallas/Ft Worth area or a city I will be visiting at some future date, I would love to meet you for lunch or an evening together.

By Telephone We can arrange an hour discussion together via speakerphone for a small gathering or large (with amplification).

On-Line Have your group compose questions for me; I will answer them all promptly. That Q&A format could serve as the basis for your next meeting.

It is easy to get started. Simply send me a note in the mail:

Leland Stewart
St. Finian's Press
11700 Preston Road
Suite 660 – 174
Dallas, TX 75230

or

An email to either of two addresses:
info@stfinianspress.com
leland.stewart@stfinianspress.com
with your comments or questions.

74789750R00190

Made in the USA
Columbia, SC
06 August 2017